"Joseph!" S
escaped her th

Joseph stopped walking and turned again to look directly into her eyes. "We will be together again," he said through clenched teeth. "Promise me you will be strong."

"Yes," Angelique sobbed. "Yes, I promise, Joseph!"

And then Joseph and Philippe were being marched onto the gangplank. Neither Joseph nor Philippe looked back again. Tears poured down Angelique's cheeks, and Marie stood like a statue by her side. Through a blur of pain, Angelique saw Joseph's hand wrap around her father's shoulder. Simultaneously, she put her arm around her mother's shoulder, although the sobs still wracked her body. She felt as though her heart would break in a million pieces.

"We must believe," her mother said quietly. "God will go with them. And He will not abandon us. Now let us go home and pray."

PEGGY DARTY is the popular, award-winning author of novels and magazine articles. Darty, who makes her home in Alabama, has been spinning wonderful tales of romance for several years—and winning awards along the way. She teaches at the University of Alabama. She is also a wife, a mother of three, and a grandmother to two little boys.

Books by Peggy Darty

HEARTSONG PRESENTS
HP143—Morning Mountain
HP238—Song of the Dove
HP273—Summer Place
HP307—Silent Stranger

Look Homeward, Angel

Peggy Darty

Heartsong Presents

For Linda Heard, soul mate and friend. Thank you for teaching me the true meaning of Christian courage.

A note from the author:
I love to hear from my readers! You may correspond with me by writing:
Peggy Darty
Author Relations
PO Box 719
Uhrichsville, OH 44683

ISBN 1-57748-753-2

LOOK HOMEWARD, ANGEL

Cover illustration by Jocelyne Bouchard.

PRINTED IN THE U.S.A.

prologue

The old woman hobbled along the cobblestone street, looking alone and out of place on a January night in Boston. The wind howled down from a black sky, snatching her dark skirts, nipping at the hood that protected her gray head. The hour was late, and most of the shops were closing now. Peering up at a sign, she turned and entered a bakery.

Only two men were inside, the owner, a sullen older gentleman, and a strikingly handsome young man. The younger man was tall with black hair and dark eyes. His smile showed even white teeth against bronzed skin.

He was smiling as the old woman entered. Glancing at the owner, whose frown merely deepened at the prospect of one last customer after a twelve-hour day, the young man stepped quickly to the counter.

"May I help you?" he asked. "Our special today is honey buns."

She nodded, peering up at him from underneath her hood.

"I will get them for you," the young man said gently.

Quickly, he removed the crusty buns from the brick oven, wrapping them carefully in brown paper, and then tied the package with a length of string. "One shilling," he said, darting a glance at the owner, whose sharp eye was ever on the lad. Money was very important to Mr. Weatherford.

The woman fumbled in her pocket and removed a worn lace handkerchief, unknotting it carefully. She removed a shilling, her last, and let it drop onto the counter.

"Thank you," the young man answered. "Do you have far to go on this cold night?"

"Only to Government Street," she muttered in a low voice, then coughed. She was obviously not well.

"Take care," he called after her as she turned slowly, the warm buns in their brown cover gripped tightly against her chest. The young man glanced at the owner.

"Lock up," Weatherford barked as he began to untie his apron.

The young man hurried to the door, shoving the bolt. Then he stepped to the back room and removed his apron and cap and placed them inside the barrel of soiled linen. He removed his worn coat from the hook on the wall, and then, hurrying now, he bid his boss good night and went out the door.

Outside, he quickly circled to the front of the shop, his heart beating fast. Down at the end of the block, he spotted the old woman, moving slowly along, and his steps quickened. He was certain now, almost entirely certain. . .

Careful to keep his distance, he followed as she turned the corner onto Government Street. Passing the tavern, he looked through the smoked window and saw only a few patrons huddled at the tables, oblivious to the street outside.

The wind picked up, sending a shiver through his gaunt body. The soles of his boots were worn thin, and he had no gloves to protect his hands. He balled them into fists and thrust them into his pockets.

The old woman had reached a house that was less affluent than its neighbors, a boardinghouse, the young man surmised. She clutched the rail and painstakingly climbed the steps leading to the front door.

He had closed the distance between them now, and in a dozen steps he could have easily reached her, but he restrained himself—waiting, waiting for the right time. His boots thudded over the cobblestones; surely she could hear him, but she did not turn around. As she opened the door, he took the stairs two at a time, reaching the front door before it closed behind her.

His eyes followed her down the narrow hallway that was lit with three candles on a small table. His eyes skimmed each closed door along the hall, counting the tiny apartments, six of them. Hers was number 7, the last one at the end of the hall.

He heard the door to number 7 open, and he crept down the hall, reaching the door just before it closed. Pushing gently on the door, he took a deep breath and then slipped inside.

The room was furnished with upturned box crates as make-do furniture. On one upturned crate was a candlestick. The old woman stood with her back to him, lighting a small candle. His breath caught in his throat, waiting for her to turn.

When she did, her brown eyes seemed to light the entire room and the face was young and radiant; the pale lips curved quickly in a blissful smile.

"Joseph!" she cried, as their eyes locked. He managed to close the door before he leapt forward. Then she was flying into his arms, toppling the hood back from her lovely face, radiant with joy.

"I thought I'd never find you," she said with a sob.

He gathered her thin body close, pressing his lips to her cold forehead. "Angelique, I never gave up," he said, as tears filled his eyes.

Her unblemished skin gleamed like polished ivory in the candle's glow. He reached for a strand of the thick hair and smiled into her wet brown eyes. "When we are old, I see that you will be as lovely as ever. Gray hair becomes you."

"The gray will wash out," she said, smiling, "but when I am gray again, I will still love you. And we will be together when we are old, we must believe that."

A noise behind him then made the young man turn to greet Angelique's mother. The three of them murmured words of joy to each other, exchanging their news. But the young man had barely said more than a few sentences when his words were interrupted by the sound of a door flung open in the house below them. British voices lifted in command as the sound of fists pounding on doors reverberated through the building.

"The soldiers," the older woman whispered, grabbing the young man by the arm. "Quickly—you must hide."

He followed her into the tiny bedroom that held only a single bed and another upturned crate with a burning candle.

"Under the bed," the woman whispered.

He dropped to the floor, flattening himself against the cold boards, attempting to fit his long body beneath the low bed.

"No, God, please," Angelique whispered, her fist pressed against her trembling lips. "Don't let them take him again!"

one

Grand Pre, Nova Scotia
October 4, 1755

Angelique Boudreau stepped out of her shingled home, the story-and-a-half saltbox typical of this tiny sea village. Market basket in hand, she tilted her face upward, studying the luminous sky, relieved to see no clouds. Beneath her white cap, her profile was lit by the sun: shining brown eyes in a delicate oval face framed with thick, dark brown hair. She was the most beautiful young woman in Grand Pre, and many were surprised she had waited until her seventeenth year to accept a marriage proposal. Now that she was betrothed to Joseph Landry, everyone approved of her choice.

Gripping her straw basket, she hurried past the lilac garden, down the rock-lined path to the cobblestone streets of the village. Automatically, she cast her eyes toward Minas Bay, inhaling the salty air that gently touched her face. The crisp air invigorated her, and on this morning her heart was bursting with happiness as she looked at the land she loved and thought of her handsome Joseph whom she would wed Sunday week. They would enrich their home with happy children and join other families who socialized at quilting bees, barn raisings, and log rollings.

Smiling to herself, she approached the market square and waved to the children swarming in a neighbor's yard. The Acadian community was filled with children, for girls married as young as fourteen and began their family in the tradition of their mothers.

"Good morning, Mademoiselle Boudreau," Monsieur Harless called from the front door of his thatch-roofed cabin.

"Good morning, Monsieur Harless. Will Joseph's coat and trousers be ready next week?" Her eyes flashed with excitement as she looked at the man who worked tirelessly as the village tailor.

"It will indeed. And a fine couple you will make."

She smiled and hurried on, her thoughts filled with Joseph and their wedding plans. A vision of the lovely white dress she and her mother had fashioned from Parisian silk and Belgian lace shimmered in her mind, and a sigh of bliss escaped her. Her mind moved on to her trousseau, and her heart beat faster as she thought of her wedding night. She had already packed away the nightgown she would wear, a soft creamy satin edged with delicate lace. It nestled in her hope chest with lilac petals from the garden.

A flush warmed her cheeks each time she allowed herself to imagine the glory of snuggling against Joseph, as his wife, while the north winds from Labrador roared across the bay. . . . Lost in her dreams, she completely missed the board step that led up to the walkway of shops.

The friendly face of one of the village women rose before her as a plump hand steadied her arm. "Daydreaming, lass?" The woman chuckled as she waddled on, her market basket overflowing with the morning's purchases.

Angelique murmured her thanks and blinked her way back to the moment. Her brown eyes tilted upward, studying the pictures that hung over the shop doors. The pictures identified the item sold within, for the majority of the village did not read. Angelique passed beneath the boot maker's sign and turned under the carving of a loaf of bread. Pressing the latch on the door, she entered the shop and was immediately warmed by the heat from the brick oven.

"Hello, Monsieur Tallese," Angelique called to the rotund man in a white apron and cap. "We are having guests for the evening meal and I have come for a loaf of your special rye."

"Ah, my favorite customer!" Round blue eyes twinkled in his flushed face. "Just for you," he said, plucking a fat loaf from the oven.

Angelique pulled the paper from her basket and handed it to him.

Carefully, he wrapped the bread, glancing back at her. "Your parents are well?"

"They are well and happy," she said brightly, unaware of the radiance that permeated her lovely face.

"Oh?" He looked at her curiously, as though he had not expected to hear this. "Ah, that we were all as happy as you, dear one."

"Why not be happy?" she asked good-naturedly. "It is a lovely autumn day. We are healthy and your business appears to be thriving." She glanced at his empty shelves.

"I fear for the future, my lass. I don't like seeing the

British ships anchored in our harbor."

"Surely you aren't worried about the rumors of trouble?" she asked.

"That I am! And the absurd reports that some of us are spies or that we consort with the Micmacs to attack the British. All lies, of course. The British have taken our weapons; next they'll be driving all the French Acadians from our homes!"

Angelique refused to believe it. Why would the British think these gentle, peace-loving farmers were a threat? True, they were French, but her people had come here to establish a settlement and build a new life for themselves and their families. They wanted no part in the disputes between England and France.

She paid for the bread and gave the baker a smile of encouragement. "Do not worry," she called over her shoulder. "Everything will be fine."

"I wish your words could be true," he said with a heavy sigh.

Angelique dismissed his pessimism as she left. She could not change the minds of others, nor had she the time to dawdle and spread cheer. She had to rush home to help her mother with the meal they were preparing for Joseph and his father. Her mother tired easily these days, for she carried the weight of an unborn baby.

Marie Boudreau was pregnant again after two miscarriages in the past ten years. Both Philippe and Angelique hovered over her constantly, endeavoring to protect her in every way. From all indications, the baby was strong and healthy. Philippe and Marie hoped for a boy who would be named Jonathan after her paternal grandfather.

As Angelique hurried down the walkway, her thoughts flew toward the cabinetmaker's shop, where she would find Joseph at work. She longed to walk the extra block just to catch a glimpse of Joseph, but her father would not approve of that. And she would see Joseph tonight.

She thought of her betrothed's strong hands, the long, tapered fingers that worked endlessly shaping, designing, building. He gave every ounce of his strength to each project, wanting to turn out perfect work, and in her opinion, he always did.

As she turned and crossed the market square, she passed a group of men assembled together in the door of a shop, their faces grim, their voices low.

". . .to meet at the church tomorrow. . .be given our orders. . ."

She sighed. More gossip. She began to hum as she hurriedly climbed the hill to their home, looking forward to the evening ahead.

❧

Joseph Landry was tall, and although he was only nineteen years of age, the muscles of his body were firm and strong from years of hard work. Pulling on his coat, he lifted his long dark hair from the collar and clasped the coat at his neck. His hair was a luxuriant black and he had never bothered with wigs as so many men did. He could not afford a wig nor did he need one; he merely styled his hair in the fashion of those who wore wigs and went happily on his way. Broad shoulders tapered to a narrow waist and long legs encased in dark trousers stretched to his ankle boots.

He glanced over his shoulder as his father entered the

living room of their small log house; the room was cluttered now with fishing net to be repaired. Charles Landry looked unusually tired tonight, and Joseph's sea-blue eyes lingered on his father's long face. Beneath a shock of white hair, his father's cheeks had a sallow color, and the lines around his eyes and mouth seemed to have deepened over the past weeks. His father was sixty years of age, still tall though slightly bent from years of labor. He had been a seaman until he jumped ship at Annapolis and married at forty to a tiny young French woman who had died giving birth to Joseph.

Joseph took a deep breath. "Are you all right?" he asked kindly. "Did you stay in your fishing boat too long this day?"

"Perhaps." His father pushed his gray lips into a smile. The blue eyes were still weary, though, and Joseph continued to wonder what ailed his father.

A thought occurred to him, although he could not believe it would be true. "Father, are you sad about my upcoming marriage?"

Charles Landry quickly shook his head. "No, my son." He clapped Joseph's broad shoulder. "Finding the right woman is God's greatest blessing. Other than the children that come from that union," he added, and to Joseph's surprise, a sheen of tears glittered in his father's eyes. "Joseph, you are the pride of my life, but I do not mind giving you up to Angelique Boudreau. I think you have selected the finest woman in Nova Scotia."

Joseph hesitated, touched by his father's words. Were those tears of sentiment, then? Was his father recalling his own wife, Joseph's mother?

Joseph gently touched his father's rough hand. "Thank you, Father. I love her more than life." He stared into his father's face, knowing he would understand.

Charles nodded. "That is the way it should be. No, my distress is over the British." Charles sighed heavily. "I fear the new governor will give our land to the British."

Joseph shook his head. "No, Father. Even though we are under British rule, we have caused no trouble; they know we are no threat."

Charles reached for his coat, nodding thoughtfully as he did. "I hope you are right, my son. Shall we go?" He tucked his snuffbox in the pocket of his coat and glanced with amusement at Joseph.

Joseph had given up snuff because of Angelique. He could not bear the thought of having snuff on his breath when he pressed his lips to Angelique's rosy mouth. She was perfect in every way, and he so wanted to live up to her expectations. He had found other women desirable, but none of them could compare to Angelique. He had lost his heart to her from the moment their eyes met in the village church, soon after he and his father arrived from Halifax.

"I am ready." He turned to his father, smoothing down his dark coat. He had thought of nothing but Angelique all day and the meal they would share tonight. All through the meal he would be able to feast his eyes upon her and dream of their wedding day.

two

Philippe, Charles, and Joseph sat by the stone fireplace in the large center room. The cooking pots had been removed, but the tantalizing smell of roasted beef still lingered in the air. Now the men relaxed after dinner, watching the flames leap merrily over the logs. Philippe had taken down his pipe and tobacco from the shelf, but tonight Charles refrained from his usual smoke. Joseph hardly noticed, however, for his attention was riveted toward the kitchen area where Marie and Angelique cleaned the pewter plates.

No matter how hard he tried, Joseph could not resist staring at Angelique; and even as she dried the plates and put them back on the shelf, her dark eyes sought his. Angelique smiled as she caught Joseph's eyes lingering on her face.

Marie intercepted the glance between the two lovers. She turned to her daughter with an understanding smile. "Go and visit with Joseph."

Angelique hesitated, looking at her mother. She searched her mother's face for signs of weariness.

Marie's hair and eyes were as dark as Angelique's, yet her face was rather plain except for the glow of happiness that lit her round face. Marie Boudreau was a sturdy country woman, a little taller than Angelique. In contrast to her mother, Angelique had tiny bones; she was a replica of her grandmother, or so she was told.

"Please rest, Mother." Angelique pressed Marie's hand.

"Yes, I will." Marie hung the cup towel on its rack. She gave her daughter a gentle pat on the cheek and then walked into the bedroom.

Angelique turned and looked at Joseph. He waited for her at the bench beside the spinning wheel, a far corner of the room that was sheltered from their fathers' gazes. She felt the blood rush through her body as she walked across the room, her eyes never leaving the face of her beloved. He reached for her arm and they sat down together, as close as possible.

As Joseph's callused fingers clasped her smaller ones, her eyes darted to her father to see if he was watching. To her relief, his head was lowered as he filled his pipe.

"The meeting will be in the village church at ten," Charles Landry said, his words coming in a rush.

Angelique noticed that his face was suddenly flushed, and she wondered if he had been into his flask of ale.

"We are like pawns in a chess game between France and England." Her father spoke gravely as he sucked on his pipe, sending a pungent aroma across the room. "Have they forgotten our endless hours of breaking rock, clearing fields, and cultivating pastures? And what about the dikes we have built to keep Grand Pre safe?"

Angelique looked back at Joseph. His dark head was inclined toward the men, and he seemed to be listening intently. She longed to lighten his mood, for their time together was precious, so she squeezed his hand. He turned to face her, and with relief, she watched his serious expression give way to a look of pleasure.

"Joseph, I'm glad you aren't talking gloom and doom like everyone else in Grand Pre." Angelique's brown eyes glowed as she looked up at him. She was so happy to be with him; all they wanted was to be together for the rest of their lives.

"And is everyone talking gloom and doom?" he asked, tilting his black head as his eyes roamed lazily over her. She was wearing a mulberry woolen dress, with a long white collar that accented the rich brown in her eyes.

"Yes," she sighed, shaking her head. "I hate seeing the worried faces and hearing silly rumors that the British might drive us from our homes to some other colony. This is the happiest time of my life, and I do not want it spoiled."

She had spoken loud enough for her father to hear. He glanced her way, and his lips gave a brief smile before his teeth clamped down on the pipe again. "Let us hope Governor Lawrence will deal fairly with us," he said on a lighter note. "Maybe the message we are given tomorrow will be one that relieves our anxieties. I suspect we will be given another curfew or a new set of laws."

He glanced back at Angelique, and she smiled her approval. Then her eyes darted to Joseph. He seemed to have dismissed the gossip as well, for his attention was riveted on her face, and she enjoyed the way he looked at her.

"In just one week, we will be man and wife," he said, speaking in a soft voice that brought a blush to her cheeks. His eyes roamed over her face, and she knew he had read her thoughts. "Soon we will be together in the new log cabin over the hill." He lifted her fingers to his lips, gently kissing each one and watching her as he did.

"Yes," she whispered, her dark eyes dancing.

Her hand moved from his lips, tracing the outline of his square jaw, gently touching the curve of his cheekbone as she absorbed each feature of his face. His hair looked blue-black in the glow of the seven fat candles illuminating the house. His eyes, darkly fringed, were a deep pure blue, probing through the layers of a person, finding the truth in one's heart. His lips were perfectly sculpted, and although he was the most handsome man she had ever seen, his soul was what she truly loved. He was a good man, kind and compassionate, honest and sincere, remarkably tender. She knew that he served God with his life, and she had no doubts that he would be a faithful husband, a gentle lover, a caring father to their children. And they had agreed to have at least four, possibly five.

Catching her father's eyes upon them, she gently withdrew her hand and dropped it to the soft folds of her woolen skirt.

Charles got slowly to his feet. "The hour is getting late, Joseph," he said. "We should go now."

Philippe stood, too, his eyes meeting those of his daughter as she looked from his face to Charles's. She detected a sense of caution about them both, as their eyes moved from her to Joseph. Angelique wondered if they thought she and Joseph should not have been sitting so close together. Did their fathers want to keep them properly separated until their wedding night?

A tiny sigh escaped her as she tilted her head up to Joseph. She wished with all of her heart that the week would magically disappear and they would never have to say good night again.

Joseph's eyes mirrored his reluctance to leave, but his long legs moved, and he stood above her. "I'll bring fresh fish for your family's dinner tomorrow night." He turned quickly to Philippe. "If you do not object, sir."

"We would enjoy that." Philippe nodded. "And of course I will see you and Charles at the meeting tomorrow."

Charles stumbled, then his arms shot out, clutching the nearest chair for support. Joseph hurried to his father's side.

"It is nothing," Charles said, waving a hand in dismissal. "A slight case of indigestion from overindulging in a wonderful meal." He straightened slowly and looked at Angelique. "Thank you. And please thank your mother for us as well." He turned to Philippe. "We have enjoyed your hospitality. I will see you tomorrow."

Philippe nodded. He smiled, but as Angelique looked at her father, she thought she saw a shadow pass over his face. His eyes moved first to her, then to Joseph, and she watched his face soften.

"Good evening, sir," Joseph told him. "Thank you for your hospitality." With a tender glance at Angelique, he turned and followed his father through the door.

Angelique's heart went with him. As her father closed the door and bolted it for the night, she felt the ache she always felt when she said good-bye to Joseph.

Again, she sighed. Her father walked toward her, saying nothing. She knew he read her face, and he smiled gently. At times, words were unnecessary between them; they were unusually close for father and daughter. The lingering aroma of tobacco tickled her nostrils, but she did not mind his habit. Tenderly, she rested her head against his shoulder.

"I will miss not having you under my roof," he said, patting her hand.

Her head tilted on his shoulder, and she studied the man who had been so good to her. Her father was not a tall man in comparison to Joseph, and yet he was similar to many other Acadians, of medium height and build. His hair was a pale brown that matched his gentle brown eyes.

"It is good to see you looking so happy," he said quietly, looking deeply into his daughter's uptilted face. She knew he must see the stars in her eyes.

"Oh, Father," she sighed, "I have never been so happy. And I will be even happier when I am Madame Joseph Landry."

He smiled and nodded. Then his eyes moved on to the bedroom door. "I must see about your mother."

As he walked away, Angelique turned and wandered toward the bench where Joseph had sat. She reached out, trailing her fingers over the smooth dark wood, as her eyes moved on to the hearth. For a long time, she stared dreamily into the fire and wished that all of Grand Pre could share the glow that overflowed her heart.

three

A thin veil of clouds overcast the morning, setting a gray mood upon the residents of Grand Pre. Angelique looked at the sky and frowned. She had followed her father to the market square on the excuse of needing more milk, because she was curious, even concerned for the first time. Besides, she was hoping to see Joseph. Even a smile and a moment's glance from him would brighten her day, and she hugged her milk pail tight against her. A pang struck her heart as she watched the procession of boys and men arriving at the village church. They all looked so solemn, as though they were on their way to a funeral. . . .

"Go home now," her father urged her, looking more grave than she had seen him in years.

She nodded, standing on tiptoe while she cast one final glance over the crowd. Joseph and his father were nowhere in sight, and her morning jaunt seemed in vain. Yet her instincts told her that she had witnessed something important. *What is going to happen?* she wondered. Surely the pall of gloom that hung over the village would be dispelled before long.

Her steps quickened on the path as her thoughts raced. Why had all the males of Grand Pre been ordered to report to the church? She had assumed only the grown men would be attending the meeting, but there had been boys there as well, young ones at that, trudging after their fathers.

Her thoughts whirled and then settled on Joseph. By now perhaps he and his father were inside the church; she wondered what he was seeing and hearing at this moment. If only she could be a tiny insect hidden in the chinks of clay that sealed the log church.

❧

The church was filled to overflowing. Once the wooden pews were packed with bodies, men and boys lined the walls, waiting. They stared with suspicion at the red-coated colonel who stood at the podium. The colonel glanced from the paper in his hand to the shuffling crowd, and for a moment, he seemed reluctant to speak. The expression in his somber eyes spoke volumes, however, and a hush of dread silenced the shuffling crowd.

Then, in the church's deep silence, he began to read the order. Each word that left his mouth fell like a stone, hammering in the message that would forever change their lives. "Without hesitation, I shall deliver you His Majesty's orders and instructions; namely: that your lands and tenements, cattle of all kinds and livestock of all sorts, are forfeited to the crown. . . ."

The silence ended. Gasps of shock sliced the air. The British officer faltered momentarily, then plunged on, his cheeks as red as the apples in the Boudreau orchard.

"With all your other effects, you are to be removed from this province. I am, through His Majesty's goodness, directed to allow you liberty to carry off your money and household goods, as many as you can without discommoding the vessels you go in. . . ."

Murmurs of disbelief rolled over the crowd; then the murmurs grew stronger, more fierce, erupting into shouts of anger.

Joseph felt the blood drain from his face, and for a split second, the sea of faces dimmed, and he heard only the hoarse shouts of outrage.

"Order!" the colonel shouted, and Joseph catapulted to his senses. Behind him there were footsteps and the cock of muskets. He turned to see that British soldiers blocked the doors of the church, their muskets lifted.

His father was yanking Joseph's sleeve, muttering protests. Numbly, Joseph forced his eyes down to meet his father's stricken face.

"What can we take?" Charles rasped. "Can we pack our homes on our backs like. . ." His work-roughened hands shot to his chest, clutching at his coat, as he gasped for breath.

"Father!" Joseph's strong arms shot out to hold his father.

Philippe whirled, shock vivid on his face. As he was focused on Charles, he quickly braced him with a hand, helping Joseph support Charles's sagging frame. Joseph's eyes darted from Philippe to the British colonel, then back to Charles.

"My father is ill," Joseph called out, but no one was listening. The roar was deafening as men shouted and shoved. A half-grown boy began to sob hysterically.

"Order!" the colonel shouted again. "There is more to hear."

For only a moment, the panic ceased. Joseph opened his mouth to yell again for help, but the colonel's words drowned him out. "I'm allowing twenty men at a time to go back to your homes in preparation for the move. But do not linger. If you do not return," his voice rose threateningly, "you will endanger the lives of your neighbors and loved ones. Families will not be separated if everyone cooperates. . . ."

Joseph turned to his father. With Philippe's help, he dragged him toward the door. The soldiers guarding the door took one look at Charles's gray face and allowed them to pass.

Tears filled Joseph's eyes as he lifted his father in his arms and carried him down the steps. His father was completely still; no breath moved his chest, and with a choked sob, Joseph acknowledged the truth. He carried his father's body across the square to a quiet patch of grass beneath a maple tree. Joseph knelt beside him and closed the lifeless eyes. Overhead, the maple's leaves spread a red canopy over the dreary scene.

Philippe knelt beside him, staring in disbelief at the body of his friend Charles. A priest found them there, and he knelt with them, praying quietly. Joseph tried to direct his thoughts toward God, but his mind felt numb and blank. He could barely comprehend what had happened. One moment his father had been with him, tugging on his sleeve—and now he was gone.

The other men who had been released from the church did not stop to offer consolation, for time was of the essence. They bolted for their horses; a few ran helter-skelter down the road. Joseph watched them dully and then his head sank.

Reluctantly, Philippe turned to Joseph as the priest

finished his prayer. "I must go to Marie and Angelique and tell them what has happened. Will you be all right?"

Joseph's dark head was still lowered, but he nodded mutely. Philippe gripped his shoulder affectionately, then stood up and ran through the crowd to the hitching rail.

Philippe mounted his horse and rode breakneck to his farm, his thoughts racing as the words of the British officer still thundered in his memory. Families would not be separated if everyone cooperated, but how could anyone cooperate with such a terrible order? How could he take his family from the farm that had been home for the past twenty years? It would be like ripping up the roots of the oaks and maples and expecting them to flourish on foreign soil.

The sky overhead was a gray blur as he rode like a wild man beneath the gold and scarlet trees, up the narrow lane that led past the new cabin for Joseph and Angelique, to his beloved home with Marie. How could he tell Marie and Angelique? How?

He jumped from his horse before the stallion had come to a halt at the hitching post. At the same time, the front door flew open. Marie stood waiting, her eyes wide with worry, her face pale. Behind her Angelique hovered, her brown eyes still holding the hopes of youth and unblemished optimism. Her face tore at his heart, for she was about to be exposed to one of the most harsh realities that life could deal them.

How could he tell them?

The question hammered at his brain with the force of anvil on steel, but then he thought of Charles Landry, and he knew the worst had not yet befallen him. He still had his health. Somehow they would survive this.

"The news was bad." Marie spoke for him. They were so close that each could read the other with a glance, and now his eyes revealed the horror that seized him. He struggled for composure; he had to be strong for his family, for his unborn child.

"Yes, the news is bad," he said, hurrying up the porch step. "But we have each other." He enveloped both women in his arms. "We must leave," he told them.

"Leave?" Marie echoed, her shocked eyes searching her husband's face.

He nodded, unable to speak.

Marie swallowed, reaching to him for support. "But why?"

"I think the British fear that we will unite with the Micmacs and incite a riot against them. Or perhaps they think we are spying for the French and that we will escape to French Canada and take up arms against them." He suddenly felt old and tired and barely able to speak. "They see us as a threat to them. This land has gone back and forth from French to British rule. We are under British rule now; we cannot rebel."

"How is Joseph?" Angelique asked in a tiny whisper as her eyes grew round and darker in her small white face.

Philippe sighed. "Joseph is all right. He will go with us. But not Charles," he added slowly, his throat tight. He prayed for strength now; he must not break down before the women. They needed his strength.

"Monsieur Landry won't go?" Angelique's mouth fell open in disbelief. "Why not?"

Philippe gripped his daughter's hand. "He became ill this morning. It was his heart, I think. He. . .has died."

"Died?" Angelique cried. She pulled free of his arms, running to the closet for her cloak. "I must go to Joseph and—"

"No!" Philippe grabbed her arm as she passed, restraining her gently. He pulled her into the circle of his arms. "You will not be allowed on the church grounds, Angelique. The British soldiers have taken command of the church. Only twenty men at a time are allowed to leave. The rest are being held captive. No women are allowed out of their homes now. I only have a short time to tell you to pack what we can take by ship. . ."

"God help us!" Maries gasped.

"Father!" Angelique tugged at his sleeve. "A man has died. Surely the soldiers—"

"You can see Joseph later," he interrupted. "You can help him more by using your head. We have to think, to plan. . ."

He looked around the living room, wondering what they could take, what they would leave. His wife's hand squeezed his. As he looked at her, he tried to restrain the tears that threatened him.

"It will be all right," she said, looking from Philippe to Angelique. "We will survive this. Tell us what we must do. Then you should return so the other men will be allowed to go to their families."

Philippe nodded, trying to organize his thoughts as they walked through the house, each staring at different objects, each wondering what they could bear to leave behind.

"Father, where are we going?" Angelique asked in a weak voice.

"I. . .don't know yet. We haven't been told. Perhaps we can reunite with our own people at some other place." He took a deep breath, trying to believe the words he offered as comfort.

"Philippe, it will be all right." Marie clutched his sleeve. "As long as we are together, we can start over, rebuild."

Philippe looked into her face. Her skin was drained of all color, and yet her brown eyes were filled with dignity and courage. How could he be less courageous than his wife? He straightened his shoulders.

"Yes, we will rebuild. Now we must think what to take. The beds. . .no, Joseph and I can build bed frames. The spinning wheel—we surely need it."

"The baby clothes," Marie said, looking toward the bedroom.

"Father, I can't believe this is happening," Angelique cried, staring into space. She was gripped in the vise of shock. "Maybe. . .what if. . .is it possible the British will change their minds?"

Philippe recalled the grave face of Colonel Winslow, heard again the glaring message that had killed Charles Landry. He closed his eyes and for a moment, his own chest began to tighten. Then he found his voice. "We must assume the edict will be enforced and act accordingly."

His eyes roamed over the living area again, and he pressed a hand to his forehead. Try as he might, he couldn't seem to make a decision about what to take.

"Philippe, let us make out a list of what we need

most," Marie spoke up. "You should return to the church to help Joseph and allow the other men to return to their families."

Philippe nodded, more grateful than ever for the woman he had married. She was the axle that held the family wheel together.

Tears were rolling down Angelique's cheeks, but Marie was dry-eyed. Philippe looked at her and felt a new surge of strength. They smiled into one another's faces and he felt their love burn brighter than ever.

"I must go now. Start packing," he said, kissing Marie.

"My wedding," Angelique mumbled, staring at her father with pleading eyes.

He had to look away. The pain in her face was unbearable. "You and Joseph can still marry," he said, looking toward the door. "The ceremony may be smaller and more brief, but you can still be man and wife."

It took every ounce of his strength to turn and walk away from his wife and daughter, but he had to be fair to the other men, and he had to help Joseph. Saying nothing more, he lifted his head and walked back out of the house and down the steps. His horse pawed the ground nervously, as though aware of the tension that crackled in the air, as thick and ominous as a rumble of thunder.

Mounting, he turned and rode back to the church. He must face the future, but dread lay heavy on his shoulders, like a cloak cast in iron. Joseph—he must think of Joseph. And with that, he kneed his horse and rode faster into the wind, while overhead the sun was lost in the clouds.

❧

Joseph tried not to think of Angelique, of their future, of the hideous orders delivered by the British; he tried to concentrate on a decent burial for his father. Somehow, he still could not grasp that his father was really dead. It didn't seem possible to him that Charles would not come walking toward him at any moment. Joseph found himself thinking of things he wanted to discuss with Charles, and even as Joseph prepared the burial, one part of his brain refused to accept the terrible reality.

Philippe had helped him dig the grave in the peaceful little cemetery behind the church. Then Joseph had been allowed to go to the cabinet shop for a wooden coffin he had recently built. His mouth twisted when he ran his hand over the smooth wood, for when he built it he had no idea it would soon be occupied by his father.

A soldier had accompanied him, saying nothing, showing no emotion. Joseph tried to remain strong, although his first impulse was to turn on the soldier and bludgeon him in retaliation for his own loss. But Joseph had heard from the men in the church that some of the British soldiers hated the French Acadians and would use any excuse to kill them. Two men, in fact, had already been shot when they defied the order and ran madly into the woods, despite the soldiers' warnings to stop. With these thoughts in his mind, Joseph was cautious with the British soldier, and he hid his pain and anger behind a flat, emotionless mask.

Still, he could not believe that the British soldiers really hated them; resented them, certainly, but hate? What had the Acadians done to inspire hatred? Couldn't the British see that they were ordinary people just like themselves? Yet the soldier at his side watched him through hard, narrowed eyes, his musket close at hand.

The priest read from his Bible at the cemetery, while a neighbor delivered the eulogy for his father's hasty funeral. Tears slid unashamedly down Joseph's tanned cheeks. He wished for a brother or sister now, someone to share the burden of grief, but there was no one to stand beside him except Philippe. He was grateful for the presence of his future father-in-law, but he longed for Angelique with an ache that weakened his body. He knew, though, that she would be unsafe on the church grounds, and he had sent word by her father for her not to come. He had to think of her safety, first and foremost. He could not bear to lose Angelique, too.

The wooden box that held Charles Landry's body was lowered into the ground, and the men shoveled dirt into the grave. The sound of metal blades striking dirt and rock droned on and on, while Joseph stood frozen in his place. At last, he forced himself to move. Wiping his eyes, he knelt and began to smooth out the mounded dirt with his powerful hands, praying all the while. At last, he felt his numb heart break within him, and he poured out his grief to God, asking for strength to bear the difficult days to come.

❧

"Mother, we must go to the church," Angelique protested, pacing the floor.

For the first time in her life, Angelique was unable to lend a helping hand when her mother needed it. She was frantic with fear and worry, and yet she knew she should be calm. It was bad enough that her mother was having to endure this hardship in her condition. Angelique knew she should be helping her do. . .something. And yet all she could think of was Joseph.

"We must do as your father instructed," Marie answered wearily. "We must think with our heads and not our hearts. We have to concentrate on what we will need most. Please, Angelique!"

Angelique stared blankly at the salt cellar her mother was thoughtfully studying. This couldn't be happening; it had to be a nightmare. Surely, she would awake in her soft warm bed and realize everything that had taken place was just one long bad dream. Watching her mother, however, she hugged her arms against her chest, feeling a chill that no fire could warm. She turned away, unwilling to face the reality of leaving the home where she had always lived.

"How can they do this to us?" she shouted, not caring if her voice shook the rafters, not caring about anything.

Her mother's fingers dug into her shoulders, spinning her around. "Stop this. You are feeling sorry for yourself; you are not thinking of others. We still have your father. . .Joseph has lost his father. Try to think of him rather than yourself."

"Oh, Mother, I am thinking of him." Angelique burst into tears again. "What will happen to the little log house we have built? Where will we be married? Where will we live?"

"Angelique, you have to be strong." Marie spoke calmly, though the color had not returned to her face since her husband had delivered the dreadful news.

Angelique blinked, gazing into her mother's face. Slowly, as though coming out of a trance, her mind stumbled forward. She would still marry Joseph. They would have a home somewhere near her parents and the new baby.

The baby! She must think of her mother's condition. Automatically, her eyes dropped to her mother's protruding stomach, and she took a deep breath. At last, her mother's words took hold, and she lifted her hands to her cheeks, wiping away the tears.

"All right, Mother, what are we taking besides the pewter plates?"

four

Joseph stood in line with the other men and boys, waiting for the guards to open the church doors. They had been closed up inside the church for three days, sleeping on pews or in aisles, their food brought in to them. No one was interested in food; all the men could think about were their families and how this terrible edict would affect their lives. Speculation was rampant, but no one knew for sure what would happen next.

Joseph had overheard the soldiers talking about grouping the men by trade. Since Joseph was a cabinetmaker and Philippe a carpenter, they had quietly agreed to stick together.

Ahead, the heavy creak of the doors brought life back to his body. He straightened his shoulders, watching the boys being herded out first; then he and Philippe would follow, along with the other men.

Once his feet touched the outer step, the sunlight hit Joseph full force and he blinked. Beside him, Philippe hesitated, as though trying to orient himself to the bright glare. The British soldiers had formed a line on each side of the walk, presenting a boundary against the families waiting in the churchyard. Joseph took a deep breath, trying to strengthen his resolve, as voices rose and fell around him.

Angelique was there; he could feel it, but he could not

bear to look into her eyes. He had to remain in control, for suddenly panic had erupted through the crowd. He could hear the voices of children screaming for their fathers, and then came the broken weeping of the women. No, he could not look toward the women; he could not bear to remember Angelique with tears on her cheeks. He would remember her as he had left her the night he had eaten supper with her family, when her brown eyes had been filled with happiness as their hearts soared with love.

❧

Angelique and Marie had come to the church two days in a row, their wagon loaded with their most prized possessions. They were ready to join their men and go. . . wherever. But now, Marie was clutching Angelique's arm, her face deathly pale, her eyes glazed with shock.

"It can't be true," she said, her voice rising in disbelief.

Angelique was too stunned to react. Joseph was marching away from her. He had not even looked in her direction. What was wrong with him? And her father. . . he had stumbled, fallen, and then staggered to his feet and moved on with the shuffling men. Suddenly, quietly, the wives and mothers fell swiftly into line opposite their men, although they were still separated by a wall of troops. Surely they would be allowed to board the ship, Angelique dared hope.

Anxiously, she glanced back over her shoulder at their wagon still underneath the maple tree. The wagon held the possessions they had planned to take; how would they get them to the ship in time? Her thoughts were spinning as she and her mother dumbly followed the crowd. Then suddenly they were there, at the shoreline, beside the huge ship.

Cries rose again as the men turned back to their loved ones. Panic surged through Angelique, and she grabbed her mother's arm.

"Hurry, Mother," she urged. "It is our only chance." They began to run toward the end of the long line, craning their necks for a glimpse of Joseph and Philippe. Desperation surged through Angelique's veins; she had to speak to Joseph, she had to see him, touch him. . . . Surely, all of this was a nightmare; in a moment he would smile down at her, clasp her in his arms, speak gently in her ear, and the nightmare would be over. . . .

Marie's breath heaved in her chest as she tried to run, but with the weight she carried, all she could do was half-trot beside Angelique as they struggled through the crowd. Old women wept and younger ones fought to break through the line. Suddenly, everyone was calling the names of their loved ones, and Angelique heard the hoarse rasp of a hundred broken hearts crying out their pain.

She had never in her life felt the kind of agony that sliced through her now as reality at last shredded her final hope. They would not be allowed to board the ship. Some of the men were already being herded up the gangplank, but she still could not give up trying to reach Joseph and her father. She managed to half-drag her mother to the end of the line, until finally they were facing Joseph and Philippe.

"Joseph," she gasped. She had barely enough breath left to speak, and her voice was little more than a whisper.

He heard her, though, and turned. Her breath caught

in her throat as she stared wide-eyed up at him. His black hair was tousled about the collar of his torn shirt; his blue eyes were bleak with despair. He seemed to be carrying his emotions in a tight grip against his heart, the way the soldiers carried their guns. She knew that inside, his heart must be breaking, just as hers was, yet despite it all, he looked strong and calm. How could he be so contained while her stomach swelled and heaved like the tides of Grand Pre?

"Where are they taking you?" she asked softly.

He shook his head. "I don't know."

Her father had turned and grasped Marie's hand. "Joseph and I will stay together," he promised, "and we will send word to you soon."

"Yes. . .yes, do that. I love you, Philippe," her mother said. Her face was still deathly pale, yet her voice was calm.

Then a soldier shoved Philippe forward, and he stumbled and fell facedown in the dirt. Joseph whirled on the soldier, ready to strike him, but a musket was pointed directly at his chest. Angelique watched him fight the rush of anger that had almost cost him his life, and then he knelt to help Philippe to his feet.

A man in the crowd turned and shouted at the soldiers. "You have lied to us! We will not be reunited with our families, after all!" Some men had apparently still held out a desperate hope that upon reaching the boat, wives and children would be allowed to join them. Angelique sighed, suddenly feeling herself age a decade.

Anger and fear surged over the crowd. "You lied to us!" Shouts erupted; a shot was fired; men scuffled. And then slowly, hopelessly, the men of Acadia accepted their fate. The long line of men moved onto the ship, their shoulders sagging.

Joseph and Philippe had turned with the other men, following them forward toward the gangplank. Angelique stared in disbelief at the back of Joseph's dark head. "Joseph!" She couldn't stop the scream that escaped her throat. A soldier whirled on her, warning her to step back.

Joseph stopped walking and turned again to look directly into her eyes. "We will be together again," he said through clenched teeth. "Promise me you will be strong."

"Yes," Angelique sobbed. "Yes, I promise, Joseph!"

And then Joseph and Philippe were being marched onto the gangplank. Neither Joseph nor Philippe looked back again. Tears poured down Angelique's cheeks, and Marie stood like a statue by her side. Through a blur of pain, Angelique saw Joseph's hand wrap around her father's shoulder. Simultaneously, she put her arm around her mother's shoulder, although the sobs still wracked her body. She felt as though her heart would break in a million pieces.

"We must believe," her mother said quietly. "God will go with them. And He will not abandon us. Now let us go home and pray."

"No, I want to stay until the ship leaves," Angelique protested, tears still streaming down her cheeks. "I want to—"

"No!" Marie's voice rose sharply. "No, we will go home and pray. That is what we must do. Now do not argue with me."

Angelique turned reluctantly, respecting her mother's wish as they pressed their way back through the weeping women and shouting children. She was locked in a tomb of agony as they sidestepped women who had collapsed in tears and children who were huddled together, their little faces white masks of terror.

Angelique and Marie dragged themselves back to their wagon, and for a moment Angelique's eyes locked numbly on the items they had carefully chosen and diligently packed. She felt her insides knot up, and she gripped the rough wood of the wagon bed, for her knees had grown weak. It would do no good to collapse in tears like the others. She had promised Joseph she would be strong. Now there was nothing left to do but return home, unpack, and wait.

❧

As they stood on the deck of the ship, Joseph turned to Philippe. "We have to keep our heads," he said. He was thinking of his own father and what the shock had done to him. He knew he must be strong for Philippe, for Angelique, and for her mother. They were his only family now, and somehow they would get through this terrible ordeal. "We will be strong for each other," Joseph said firmly. He could feel Philippe trembling now, as they stood close together. Joseph vowed not to weaken, for he knew how desperately the Boudreaus needed him to be strong and calm.

❧

"We forgot to bank the fire in the hearth," Marie said as they entered the still house. Already the loneliness seemed to be a human presence, mocking them, waiting to swoop down and rob them of all hope.

"Mother, you must go lie down," Angelique insisted. As her eyes moved over her mother, really seeing her for the first time in hours, she grew concerned. Marie's shoulders were bent slightly, and she had been holding her abdomen for some time. "I will get a fire going," Angelique said, fighting another wave of fear, this time one for her mother's health. Marie nodded and walked slowly to her room.

Angelique hurried to the hearth to get the metal tinderbox. As she opened the box and removed a charred shred of linen, she tried not to think about the scene they had just witnessed. She pulled out the flint and steel and set the candle in the socket of the lid. *I will be strong,* she reminded herself.

I will be strong. In the weeks to come, the words were to become a litany to her, but for now they were still new. She sucked in a breath, strengthening her resolve, and then she held the chunk of flint in her left hand and carefully struck a glancing blow with the steel.

She made a dozen attempts before the sparks finally came, and she cautiously held her hands over the tinderbox. When a spark touched the rag, she began to blow on the tiny glitter of light, nursing it into a single flame. Her hands were shaking with cold by the time the fire took hold, and she transferred the fire to the kindling in the fireplace. After another five minutes, however, she at last had a weak little fire going. She patiently poked at it, urging the flame to lick over the small pieces of wood and finally grab hold.

Sighing with relief, she put the tinderbox away and

went to the kitchen for a cloth to clean her hands. Then she went back to the fire and sank down in the chair by the hearth, trying to absorb what had happened. It was so cruel, so unfair, but she must cling to the promise she had made to Joseph. She would not give up hope; she would be reunited with him and her father. In the meantime, she had her mother to consider and the baby that would be born.

The shock of what had happened might send her mother into premature labor. Then what would Angelique do? Panic threatened to envelope her for a moment, but she shook her head firmly and pushed it back. If her mother went into labor, then Angelique would run for the midwife, of course.

With God's help, somehow they would manage. She murmured a prayer, asking for strength and courage and protection for them all. And then she stared into the flames for a long time, trying to imagine the future without Joseph and her father.

five

The dark ocean rolled below him as Joseph stood on the deck of the ship, staring into the night. They had been at sea for days, and now men were getting sick and dying. Joseph and Philippe shared a tiny compartment with another man. Since he was the youngest, Joseph had given Philippe and the other man the bunks, and he had taken the floor. Now, at midnight, he still could not sleep, while Philippe snored in exhaustion. The other man writhed in pain. *Is he seriously ill or just seasick?* Joseph wondered. In either case, he could do nothing for the man except offer up a prayer for him.

As the minutes slipped by, Joseph still could not relax enough to fall asleep. At last, in desperation, he got to his feet. He cast one last glance at the other man's flushed face before he slipped out of the cabin.

A British officer rushed up to him, his gun pointed at Joseph.

"Please allow me to go up on deck," Joseph humbly asked. "The worst I can do is jump into the water and try to swim back to shore. And we both know that is impossible."

The guard shrugged indifferently and allowed him to pass.

On deck, Joseph lifted his eyes to the sky and took a deep breath. He had not seen the sky for many days, and now he felt a sense of relief; some of his tension eased a little. A north wind ruffled a tiny cloud away from the moon, and it shone down brilliantly, as though offering hope and promise.

But then Joseph's shoulders sagged as any sense of hope ebbed away. His father was buried back in Grand Pre, and he had been wrenched from the woman he loved with all of his heart. He had no idea where he and Philippe were going or what would happen to them. His control over his own life was totally gone.

Still, he reminded himself, he had urged Angelique not to give up hope—had asked her to promise, in fact. And now he vowed in his heart that no matter where the British took him, no matter what they did to him, someday, somehow, he would find Angelique again.

"You were coughing back in port," the voice of a British officer raged. "Why didn't you tell us you were sick?"

Joseph jumped and then realized that the officer was not speaking to him. He turned and looked down the deck to a group of officers huddled about their commander; they were all staring at the man hanging over the rail. He was clearly miserably sick. One officer turned him around and thrust a lantern in his face.

Joseph's eyes widened as he looked at the sick man; he suddenly understood what was going on, and he shuddered at the sight of the dreaded red spots on the man's face. The pox! The man had the pox and now probably others on the ship had already caught the horrible disease.

He heard the officers mutter that some of the Acadians

had fallen sick; a few had even died. Joseph's heart was as heavy as a stone in his chest. He tried to pray, but he found himself wondering why God was treating them this way. Surely, their community had done nothing to deserve such terrible punishment.

The commander turned then and stared at Joseph. "Hey, you! You are a tall strong man. We have a job for you. You are ordered to locate the dead men on board and throw their bodies over."

The commander whirled on his men. "We need to free the ship of contagion. We'll have to dock at the first available port."

❧

The days that followed seemed to never end, and the nights were even worse. One night, Joseph stood alongside two other men from Grand Pre, strong like himself, and together they silently wept as they watched their neighbors go quickly to their deaths. Joseph had heard stories about the pox, but he had never realized how furiously it raged through a person's body. The British no longer cared about the Acadians; they were concerned only with saving themselves from the contagion.

Joseph checked on Philippe frequently. He was not surprised when the other man in their compartment had died, but his heart sank as he saw that Philippe, too, seemed desperately ill now.

"You must not give up," Joseph urged. "Not everyone is dying. Some of the men have survived."

Later, when the dark waters raged and all attention was drawn to manning the ship, Joseph was bold enough to grab a container of safe water when the cook's back was turned. He sneaked the water to Philippe, taking only a small sip for himself.

He knelt beside Philippe, and gripping his shoulder, he began to pray:

"God, You have promised in Your word that if we will follow You, if we act like Your people, You will hear our cry for mercy and heal our land. I ask You now, in the name of Jesus Christ who came to save us, who bore the lashes of the whip for our healing, to heal Philippe Boudreau of this disease."

For a long moment, Joseph struggled with his doubt and despair. Slowly, though, a sense of peace stole over him. "I believe it is done," he finished quietly. "I believe You have healed Philippe." Joseph opened his eyes and looked at the feverish man.

He had prayed with conviction, claiming the victory for Philippe. In biblical times, the sick had been healed. God still had the power to save Philippe, and somehow Joseph was gripped with the conviction that He would.

He did not question now why God had allowed his father to die, but with all of his heart, he believed it was God's will for Philippe to be restored to good health. For some reason, his father's time had come to go to God—but surely this was not Philippe's time. He had a wife and daughter who needed him, as well as Joseph; without him, Joseph was not sure he would have the courage to continue to be strong. Besides, Philippe had done so much good for his neighbors; the entire Acadian community needed him, particularly now, in this time of crisis. *No,* Joseph thought, *God must surely realize that this man's goodness cannot be spared, not now, not yet.*

Joseph felt a shiver of fear run over him as doubts overtook him once more, but then he again felt the comforting touch of God's peace. Philippe would be healed.

Joseph heard shouts then from the upper deck. With a sigh, he slipped back to his job, to see what was happening.

On deck, he found a scene of confusion. "Only a few will be going ashore," a British officer was yelling at a little man, who had apparently begged to get in the small boat that had just arrived. He was the mapmaker in their community, Joseph recognized, a nasal-voiced man who was always complaining about something. Joseph had never particularly cared for him, but now as he saw the desperation in the man's eyes, his heart went out to him.

Then Joseph's gaze flew to the distant shoreline. The first light of dawn lit the eastern sky, and the ship was nearing land. Medical help would soon be available.

"Another boat will be sent back for others," the officer continued.

"But you must take me now," the short man said, his face flaming red around the ugly blisters that covered his skin. "I know something. Something important. If you will see that I get to a doctor, I will tell you."

"What could you possibly have to tell me?" the officer snarled at him. "You know nothing about the pox, or you would have saved yourself."

"Your own people tried to plant a spy on ship," the man shouted, tugging at the officer's arm.

His words seemed to be magnified a hundredfold, despite the slashing waves and the coughing sick men.

A stunned silence hung for a moment over the ship.

"A spy?" The officer turned back to him. "How do you know this?"

"Because I was to be the spy. But I refused to go along with the plan."

Joseph stared wide-eyed at the sneaky little mapmaker who should never have been trusted. But someone had trusted him, and now that person would be in grave danger wherever he or she was.

"Come below," the officer said, his eyes narrowed. The coward gratefully followed.

A musket prodded Joseph's shoulder. "Get back to your job. There are four more bodies to be tossed overboard."

Joseph went back to his task, but he was terrified now, wondering what name the mapmaker would give the British. It would be someone back home, he surmised, someone who might even now be trying to help Angelique and Madame Boudreau. They, too, would be in more danger.

A shot rang out from below. The officer beside him said with grim satisfaction, "The coward wasted his information. He got what he deserved."

six

On a dreary Saturday morning, Angelique stood staring out at the misty rain. She was sick with worry for her mother, but she had no idea what to do. For the past two days, Marie had taken to her bed, scarcely able to get up. The baby was not yet due for three weeks, but her mother had been plagued with a constant backache; she looked pale and was obviously weak. Yet she stubbornly refused to see the new British physician in Grand Pre.

"He will not touch our child!" she had stormed at Angelique when she suggested going for the new doctor. Marie planned to have the baby at home with the help of a local midwife, a Swedish woman named Olga.

Olga had married Monsieur Harless, the tailor, and moved here to Grand Pre five years before. She was a kind and competent woman, and yet Angelique worried that Olga's knowledge would be insufficient to help Marie. Angelique feared that something was seriously wrong with her mother, something for which a midwife would have no cure.

But when she voiced her concerns, her mother only shook her head. "That doctor is one of the same people who have taken our homes and loved ones," Marie reminded her, as though Angelique could possibly have forgotten such an important thing.

"Not our homes," Angelique reminded her gently. She did not voice the silent thought that followed: *Not yet.*

But they both knew that as soon as the baby was born and the women were able to travel, they, too, would be deported, just as most of the other women and children had been. The delay would work to their advantage, they prayed, for before they had to leave their home, they hoped to learn the whereabouts of Philippe and Joseph.

Each morning when she awoke, Angelique said a prayer and struggled to put their lives into God's hands. Still, each day was like an eternity for her. They were prisoners on their own land—but at least, as she had just reminded her mother, they had not been driven from their home, unlike so many other French Acadians.

Some of the British who had lived in Grand Pre for years and knew her family had persuaded the soldiers to take pity on the Boudreau women. They spread the word that Marie, greatly respected in the village, was due to have a child soon. For now, at least, they were safe in their own home.

But Marie needed help. Angelique could avoid that knowledge no longer. She turned from the rain beyond the window, wondering to whom she should turn for help.

Monsieur Tallese, the rotund little baker, had suffered a stroke on the day of the announcement in the village church. The British had allowed him to return to his home, expecting him to die. He was bedfast, his right side paralyzed and his mind stricken, yet somehow he had survived.

Childless, with most of their friends gone, Lewis and Madeline Tallese would be unable to rebuild a life for themselves elsewhere, not this late in their lives. Their building had been seized by the British, but Madame Tallese had pleaded with them to allow her to remain and pay rent. Now Madame Tallese had to try and eke out their living through the bakery.

With Madame Tallese in mind, Angelique slipped to her mother's room and peered in the doorway. Marie appeared to be asleep, at last.

Quickly, Angelique reached for her mother's dark cloak, for it would be longer on her than her own and it was hooded. For her trip to the baker, she hoped to conceal herself, for she had heard that the soldiers were rude to Acadian women.

This day should have been the day before her wedding, she realized, a day that would have been filled with joyful preparation. Instead, here she was, slipping furtively to the bakery, while Joseph and her father were far away. She cried throughout each night, heartsick with disappointment and longing, taking care to muffle her sobs into the pillow so as not to disturb Marie in the adjoining bedroom.

Huddled into the cloak, the wind felt pleasantly chilly, despite the mist and rain. She had been inside for so many days in a row that she welcomed the fresh air. This was the time of year when she usually went for long walks, because soon it would be November when frost would bite the air, and after that would come the deep snow. Now she sucked in a deep breath of relief, glad to at least be out of the house.

She found the village's narrow streets thronged with people. With the big cloak wrapped around her, though, its hood low on her forehead, she doubted she would be noticed as she slipped through the crowds.

The sound of British voices rang in her ears, and she sank her teeth into her bottom lip. She and her mother prayed nightly for Joseph and Philippe, but Angelique also added her own silent prayer: She prayed that God would keep their hearts strong and free of hatred. Resentment and frustration tugged at her heart now, but she knew that allowing her feelings to turn into hatred would do no good. More than anything, if they were to survive, they must depend upon God's strength—and Angelique sensed that if she allowed herself to hate the British, her hatred would come between her and God. Their situation was bad enough as it was; hatred would only make it worse.

Nevertheless, gloom settled over her, as dark as her mother's heavy woolen cloak. She forced herself to search for a positive side to this day, and at last thought grimly, *At least I have been spared rain on my wedding day. And from the look of the thick clouds, tomorrow will be worse.*

She would not have wanted to marry in the rain, a bad omen, she decided as she quickened her steps, but the thought brought her little comfort. She dared not look in the direction of the little church where she would have been married or at the adjoining cemetery where Charles Landry was buried. Her throat was raw with the ache of holding back the sobs that seemed forever lodged there.

With a sigh, she forced herself to turn under the baker's sign and open the door.

The bell jingled, as always, but the first thing she noticed was that the bakery felt cold, despite the heat of the oven. She spotted Madame Tallese at the long counter, busily kneading a huge ball of dough. The woman's shoulder blades jutted through her dress, telling Angelique that she had lost a good deal of weight since Angelique last saw her.

Madame Tallese merely glanced in Angelique's direction when the doorbell jingled. But another voice rang out. "Angelique, is that you?"

Angelique turned toward the end of the counter where she saw Olga, the large Swedish woman. Quickly, Olga came around the counter and rushed toward Angelique, her arms extended. Angelique saw the concern in her warm blue eyes.

"Oh, lass, you and your mother have been heavy on our hearts," she said, enveloping her in a massive hug.

Grateful for support, Angelique leaned into the woman's thick comforting arms. Olga's apron was redolent with cinnamon and brown sugar, and breathing the familiar kitchen scents, Angelique swallowed hard. She had encouraged her mother to eat the fish they had preserved, along with the vegetables neatly stacked on the pantry shelves for the winter—but Angelique hadn't had the energy or the desire to bake any sweets. Even if she had, Marie would have bypassed them in order to choke down the basic foods she needed to keep the baby healthy. But now the sweet scents made Angelique's mouth water and filled her with sudden longing.

"My dear." Madame Tallese left her dough and came forward. "I did not realize it was you. But take care." The weary eyes flicked over Angelique's shoulder to the narrow window overlooking the street. "They are accosting women on the streets," she lowered her voice, "and you should not go out unless you are well disguised."

"Yes, yes," Olga quickly agreed, tugging the hood

lower on Angelique's head.

"I will remember that," Angelique replied. "Thank you. Please tell me; how is Monsieur Tallese?" She felt a wave of sympathy for the couple. Madame Tallese looked so small, so bereft.

The question was like a physical blow to the woman. Her face crumpled as her shoulder slumped forward, as though a barrel of whale oil had just been cast upon her small back. She whirled back to the counter, unable to reply.

"He is still quite ill," Olga whispered, pushing a strand of gray-blond hair away from her round face. "But he is slowly improving. I am helping Madeline here in the bakery." The concern in her eyes was clear as she glanced toward the woman whose back had straightened once again while she methodically went about her tasks.

Angelique watched Madame Tallese thoughtfully, wondering how she could continue to function after such terrible sorrow had struck her life. Suddenly, Angelique realized that Madame Tallese had survived by keeping her mind focused on her work; obviously, the woman was shutting everything else out of her thoughts so that she could keep going with what she had to do. Angelique regretted now her question about Monsieur Tallese's health, even though she had voiced it out of concern.

Angelique's eyes skimmed over the trays spread on the racks. Once Monsieur Tallese would have done most of this work, particularly the heavy lifting. She looked back at Olga. "It is kind of you to help," Angelique said quietly. "I'm sure she needs you."

Olga nodded, gripping Angelique's gloved hand. "How is your dear mother?"

"Not well," Angelique sighed, sinking to the nearest wooden bench.

Wordlessly, Madeline wrapped a loaf of bread in brown paper and handed it across the counter to Angelique, along with a warm package that smelled of sweet rolls.

"Thank you," Angelique murmured, unable to stop the tears.

Madeline turned quickly as though she could not bear to look at Angelique for another second.

"You say your mother is not well." Olga studied Angelique's lowered head, watching the tears trickle down her cheeks.

"I'm glad you are here." Angelique's voice trembled. "I fear we will be needing you soon." She raised her wet brown eyes to Olga, eyes that were huge with worry and fear.

Olga patted her shoulder with a large, gentle hand. "And I will come. If you cannot reach me at the house, my husband is free to come and go. Get word to him. He has been allowed to stay in business because—"

"Yes, I know," Angelique interrupted. Olga's husband was British and had pledged allegiance to the throne. Angelique's voice dropped to a whisper. "Someday Joseph will wear the suit your husband has made for him."

Olga smiled sadly as Angelique stood up, gripping the packages Madame Tallese had given her. Angelique couldn't bear to say anything more. She was agonized even thinking of Joseph, imagining how he would have been dressed in his new suit, waiting at the altar of the church, waiting to make her his wife, so their lives could be joined forever. . . .

Olga stepped closer to her, her voice a gentle whisper

in Angelique's ear. "We have a spy on the ship. He will report to us as soon as the men are deported someplace. I will know the place, and then you and your mother can slip away and join them."

Angelique's head jerked up, her heart soaring in a way she never thought possible again. "God bless you," she whispered.

Her gaze followed Olga's warning gaze toward the street, and she fell silent. Still, her heart overflowed with joy at the encouraging words Olga had just spoken. Her arms flew around Olga's ample waist, hugging this dear wonderful woman who had dared to help them. Surely Monsieur Harless would help all of them to be reunited.

"She should go," Madeline barked from behind them.

Quickly, Olga released her and stepped back to the counter just as the door opened. "Come in, sir," she said. "The sweet rolls are just now out of the oven."

Angelique turned so quickly that she almost bumped into the red sleeve of the British soldier. A group of soldiers filed in behind him, and one even had his weapon drawn. All looked serious, their faces heavy with anger.

Angelique slipped past the soldiers, glad to escape the tension in the air. She wondered what had happened. From inside the shop, she could hear the officer's voice raised in a loud command. What did he want? What was wrong? She lowered her head and began to walk faster.

The rain was coming down harder now, and fewer people were along the street. Most had gone inside the shops, save for the Redcoats with their guns, who were stationed on every corner.

Her heart beat faster, but she forced herself to slow

down, to lean forward, to try to recall the way an old woman walked. She had almost reached Monsieur Harless's house, when thunder crackled, and a sudden blast of wind shook her, whipping the hood from her head. Her long black hair flew about her shoulders, whipping her face, and she walked faster again, her hand flying over her head to capture the elusive hood.

Suddenly, a firm hand clasped her wrist. She was whirled about and pulled under the overhang of a shop roof.

"What have we here?" asked the voice that belonged to the firm hand.

Her eyes crept up the red uniform to the thick lip that curled sardonically as he spoke. Immediately, her eyes skittered back to the package she clutched tightly. A gloved hand jerked her chin up so that she was looking directly into a pair of bloodshot blue eyes. They swept down her cloak.

"This has to be the one," he said to his companion. "The beauty of Grand Pre, she is said to be. Left here to take care of her sick mother. What is your name?" he barked, his bulging chest vibrating with the depth of his voice.

She swallowed, trying to still the trembling of her lips to form a reply. Before she could speak, his hand reached out to rip the wet cloak open, revealing her simple brown dress.

"Yes, she is the one," he confirmed with an ugly laugh. "The figure matches the face—in fact, I've not seen such a woman as this in a very long time. Too long."

"Please," she managed to plead, "my mother is very sick. Please, sir, allow me to return home to her."

"But of course. In fact, I will see you home." He

motioned for a carriage.

"Careful," a soldier said in a low voice. "We just got orders to—"

"Never mind," the officer cut him off. He opened the door of the carriage.

Angelique's eyes darted toward the tailor's shop. If only she could get to Monsieur Harless, if only. . . But then an arm swung around her shoulders, the fat fingers biting through the cloak. She felt as though her heart had stopped beating, while her skin crawled, and her blood seemed to freeze solid in her veins.

"Get in," he ordered.

She could see no alternative, so she did as he said.

He hauled himself into the buggy, making a whooshing sound as his considerable bulk settled beside her. In the small interior, he smelled of rain and cold and bad breath. Angelique was shaking so that she could hardly hold on to the bread.

A shot rang out from somewhere behind them, reminding Angelique of the danger that enveloped all of Grand Pre. She was not the only one in danger, and she breathed a prayer for them all. Then the carriage door was slammed, and the horses set off at a trot.

Angelique clasped her trembling hands together, unable to think what to do. She was only sure of one thing: She could not anger this man, and so she gave her address to him through trembling lips. He yelled directions to the driver.

The face of her beloved Joseph flashed through her memory. If he could see her now, his eyes, the beautiful blue eyes that had turned as dark as a January night the only time she had seen him angry, would be dark now.

He would be beyond anger if he knew what was happening here.

She had to survive for Joseph; she had promised him. Otherwise, she feared she would take her life now, however she could. But of course that would be a cowardly thing to do. There was her mother to consider, and the baby. And maybe someday she would be reunited with Joseph again. Somehow God would see to that. She clung to that belief like one drowning in the icy waters of Minas Bay, like one reaching for the lifeline from a ship hand.

Having no idea what she would tell her mother, she alighted from the carriage with the bread and the smashed package of sweet rolls and hurried up to the house.

"A lovely little abode," the ugly man commented as he followed her.

"Please." She turned pleading eyes to him as they approached the front door. "Do not bother my mother."

"That will be up to you," he said coldly.

She opened the door and called out, "Mother, I'm home."

A cry of agony answered her. "Hurry. Help me!"

Without any thought of the officer behind her, Angelique dropped the bakery items on the table and rushed into her mother's room.

Marie had lit a small candle, and by its light Angelique saw her mother sitting on the side of the bed, clutching her stomach. Her abdomen looked like a huge ball to Angelique.

"Mother. . .are you in labor?"

Marie's eyes moved past Angelique and widened in alarm. Angelique glanced around to see the officer standing in the door, witnessing her mother's condition.

"Who are you?" Marie gasped.

"Mother, do not be concerned." Angelique patted her mother's hand. "He gave me a ride home. That is all."

But Marie was gripped with another contraction, and she responded with a scream that sent the man fleeing from the doorway.

"I will go for help," Angelique said, kneeling beside her mother's bed. "But first we must pray."

She struggled to shape her desperate thoughts into words. At last she managed to whisper, "Dear God, be merciful unto her." Then she jumped to her feet and rushed back into the living room. The door had opened and the officer was already leaving. God had already answered one of her prayers at least.

For a moment, she considered following the officer and asking him for a ride back to town, but she knew she had been saved from a terrible fate. She would get help on her own and be rid of the officer rather than risk putting herself in danger once more.

She stepped back into her mother's room and touched her shoulder gently. Her mother stared up at her with wild eyes. "Is he gone, Angelique? That man. . .?"

"He is gone," Angelique assured her. "Mother, I need to go get Olga."

"No," her mother said, her face lined with weariness. "Not yet. The pains are not regular yet, and they are still too far apart. Wait, Angelique. . . ." Marie slumped back on the bed, her eyes falling shut.

❧

Angelique stayed by her mother's side all through the long day that followed and into the night. The pains came and went, and her mother's face grew gray with weariness. *Please, God,* Angelique prayed as she wrapped her arms around her mother's shoulders, bracing her against yet another contraction, *let this baby come soon. Mother cannot endure this much longer. She will be too tired to deliver the baby. Please, God. . .*

At last, as morning dawned, the contractions became regular. When they were fifteen minutes apart, Marie clutched Angelique's hand. "It is time," she breathed.

Angelique jumped to her feet. "I will return with Olga."

Her mother nodded. "Please be careful," she gasped as another pain gripped her.

Angelique put on her mother's dark cloak once more. She wound her hair back and tied it in a knot, then pulled a woolen scarf over her head, tying it sturdily under her chin. This time, she would take no chances with the wind or the rude soldiers.

Angelique flew through the small house and stepped out into the brisk gray air. The acrid smell of smoke filled the air, and she wondered if one of the remaining merchants had torched his business rather than have it taken over by the British. A Redcoat glanced at her suspiciously as she made her way toward town, and she forced herself to pace her steps and hunch forward. Walking like an old woman, she hobbled down the path to the village.

She could hear shouts and gunshots rang out. Her gaze jerked up from the rocky path, and then her breath caught in her throat as she spotted one of the tavern owners, a sympathizer in the French-Indian wars. He was standing helplessly in the street as his home went up in flames.

Red uniforms were everywhere, and an even worse possibility occurred to her: Were the British deliberately burning the buildings? Were they destroying the town on purpose?

The Harless home was just around the next turn. Would Olga be there at this early hour or already at the bakery? The Harless's house was nearest, and Angelique decided to try there first. She lowered her head, forcing each step to be slow and awkward, while her heart raced and her mind was wild with panic. Only a few more steps and she would make the turn down the cobblestone street to Olga's house. She heard gunfire again, and she dared walk faster. Then to her horror, she saw the source of trouble.

British soldiers filled the Harless's tiny yard, tromping over Olga's flower beds. In the center of the yard. . .

Her hand flew to her mouth to stifle a scream. Monsieur Harless was hanging from the tree, his body limp, his face lowered in death.

A throng of people had gathered in the street, and Angelique crept to the back of the crowd, more terrified than she had ever been.

"All of you see what will happen to spies," a soldier shouted. "This couple dared defy us. Let that be a lesson to anyone who would dare be a traitor. You will die as these two have."

Tears blurred Angelique's vision, as she turned slowly, knowing she must get away before anyone spotted her. Later, her mind would take in the awful scene she had just witnessed, try to make sense of the words she had heard, but for now she must keep her mind on her own safety. Otherwise, she would not be able to return to her mother. Her mother needed her. . . .

Her mother! Without Olga's help, what would she do?

Angelique stopped walking, her eyes frantically running over the crowd. Here and there she saw a woman she recognized, someone who had been left behind for one reason or another when the others were deported. Each woman's face was pale, and they were obviously frightened half to death. Angelique knew that no one in this crowd would dare to move, to do anything other than be marched back to their homes and remain there under guard.

She hobbled on, coughing as she passed a soldier, a handkerchief pressed to her mouth. What would she do? To whom could she turn? She prayed for guidance, and a thought came to her.

Madame Russo was their nearest neighbor, and she was still in her house. She was French by birth, but she had refused to go live with her only daughter in Boston when the daughter and her husband had come for her this summer. Instead, they had agreed their son could remain with his grandmother until November, when they would return for both him and Madame Russo. The old woman had often proudly told Angelique and her mother that her grandson had inherited his grandfather's love for the sea. Angelique remembered seeing him down at the wharf, watching with wide-eyed fascination as the men unloaded their lobster pots. The grandfather who had loved the sea had died there, going out into a storm after lobsters once too often, but his grandson was apparently undaunted by the tragic family story.

Angelique shivered now within her cloak, her eyes fixed on the cobblestones at her feet. So many families had been torn apart during this time; now even an innocent little boy could not return to his parents. His father was British, so perhaps the Redcoats would let him through the barricade. He was a silversmith, Angelique remembered, so he would have money; perhaps he would be able to bribe the British officers. She was certain that one way or another he would come for his son and mother-in-law once he heard of the crisis here, and when he did, perhaps he could help Angelique learn the whereabouts of Joseph and Philippe.

She drew hope from that thought, and she took a deep breath. Her thoughts turned to her present need. If only Madame Russo could midwife the baby. . . .

Angelique's thoughts raced as wildly as her heartbeat. All around her, everyone's attention was centered on the gruesome scenes taking place. No one seemed to care about the sick old woman she pretended to be. She dared walk a bit faster, limping as she did, and after what seemed an eternity, she reached the gate of her neighbor's dark house. Madame Russo and her grandson were apparently still in bed, perhaps too terrified to leave their home. They must have smelled the smoke and heard the noise and confusion everywhere.

Angelique hurried to the door and rapped gently against the cold wood, calling Madame Russo's name softly. The door remained closed. Angelique tried the knob. Locked. She looked around and saw that the shutters were closed, but she could feel the warmth seeping from under the door. They were at home.

She hurried around the one-story, shingled house to the side window and began to knock on the tiny pane. "Madame Russo?" she called out, as loudly as she dared.

Finally, the boy appeared at the window, his hair tousled, his young face filled with questions.

"It is Angelique, your neighbor," she called to him. "Please open the door and let me in."

He nodded and disappeared from the window, and she hurried back to the front door. Shivering inside the cloak, she waited for the key to rattle in the lock.

Slowly the door opened. The room was dark behind the boy's sleepy face.

"I must speak to your grandmother," Angelique said, pushing her way past him.

"She is not well," he protested, lighting a candlestick near the door.

Angelique's heart sank at his words. "But I need her help," she told the boy. She blinked against the shadows, waiting for her smoke-filled eyes to adjust to the wavering dim light of the candle.

"Your. . .your name," she stammered. "I must have forgotten. . ."

"I am Claude," he answered, leading the way toward the small dark room where Angelique could hear the heavy snores of the old woman.

"Grandmere," he whispered, creeping to the side of the bed, the candlestick hoisted high in his hand.

Angelique followed, then frowned. The woman was an ashen gray; she was obviously very sick. How could she possibly help?

Claude gently touched Madame Russo's shoulder. "Grandmere, wake up."

The white head rolled on the pillow. Her wrinkled face looked drawn and withered, but at last the watery eyes opened and narrowed on her grandson's face. Her gaze moved past him then to Angelique.

"Madame Russo, it is Angelique Boudreau." Angelique knelt beside the bed, shocked at how the woman had deteriorated in just the past month.

"What. . .why are you here?" Madame Russo asked, first blinking, then squinting up toward Angelique. She seemed to be in a daze.

"I fear my mother is about to have the baby, and there is no one to help me," Angelique explained quickly. "Olga. . ." She broke off, unable to break the shocking news to this woman.

"Marie is in labor?" Madame Russo pushed her thin body up halfway in the bed, then sank back against the pillow. "I do not feel so well. You are the daughter of Marie?"

"Yes; can you possibly come help me?"

The old woman's hand flailed out, seeking Angelique's, and Angelique froze as she felt the woman's icy touch. She looked into her rheumy eyes, and with despair, she realized the woman was nearly blind.

"I can do nothing but lie abed and suffer. But Claude. . . Claude can go for Olga." The old woman sank deeper into the pillows, as though the small effort had exhausted her.

"It. . .is not safe to go into the village," Angelique said, trying to keep the fear from her voice. "Can you think of someone closer?"

"What's that?" Madame Russo asked, frowning up at her. "I don't hear so well."

Staring at the helpless woman, Angelique realized there was nothing Madame Russo could do to help.

Claude spoke up from behind her. "I will fetch someone for you," he said, standing erect and proud, obviously the little man of the house.

Angelique turned and studied his features for the first time. She remembered he was small for his age but very bright. "How old are you?" she asked.

"I am ten, but I told the British officers that I was nine. I would not make the boat voyage because of Grand-mere. She was too sick to go, and she needed me."

Angelique smiled gently and reached out to touch his narrow shoulder. "It is good that you did." She beckoned him into the other room. As they stood in the living room, lit only by the single candle, Angelique glanced frantically out the window. Should she tell him what was going on in the village? She decided it was only fair that he know; soon the soldiers might be knocking on their door.

"I must tell you some things, but I cannot stay long." She sank onto the nearest bench, pulling the scarf from her head and trying to catch her breath.

"I smelled the smoke. What is happening in the village?" he asked.

As quickly and quietly as possible, she told him exactly what she had seen, regretting the fear she saw in his eyes as he heard the story. But she had to be honest. He seemed to be mature for his years and he must be warned. When she had finished the gruesome story, her mind flew back to her mother. Angelique had been gone too long. She needed to get home.

"Can I fetch someone for you?" the boy asked, quickly summing up the situation and seeing her despair.

"I. . .don't know. The soldiers are everywhere. Perhaps . . .perhaps you could come back home with me, and if Mother is better, then we can wait until later in the morning. Then you can go to the village and find help for me."

"Yes, I will do that. Let me tell Grandmere I am going to help you."

"Are you going to tell her about—?"

He shook his head. "There is nothing she can do but worry and grow weaker," he answered and then hurried back to the old woman's bedroom.

Watching his small frame move quickly toward his grandmother's room, Angelique marveled that the little boy seemed so wise and capable.

Soon he was back, wearing his woolen coat and dark tam. "I am ready now." He blew out the candle.

Pulling the scarf over her head, Angelique forced her thoughts back to what must be done. It was another ten-minute walk to her house, and she had been gone for over an hour. She was filled with a sudden frantic desperation to be home with her mother.

Silently, they hurried through the back meadows, taking the most obscure path so as not to be seen. Angelique's heart was filled with foreboding. What, she wondered, would they find at her house?

seven

They were walking together in a green meadow, he and Angelique. Joseph could hear the seagulls call as they dipped and swayed in the soothing breeze off Minas Bay. The air slipped across the meadow and caught a lock of Angelique's dark hair, laying it across a rounded cheek. Her cheek was soft and warm beneath his fingers as he pushed her silky hair back in place. She was laughing, the wonderful light sound that was always music in his ears. He was laughing, too, as he held her small hand in his, their fingers entwined. Her head was tilted back and her slim nose and soft mouth begged to be kissed, but he could wait. Wait until Sunday, when they would claim the cabin their hands had built. . .

They walked up the slight incline, where violet-colored crocuses spread a sea of deep purple before them. A path ran through the trees and they took it under the grove of apple trees in full bloom. Marie and Angelique would gather and preserve the apples; like her mother, Angelique had learned to bake the thick brown-crusted pies that were Joseph's favorite.

"The cabin will go there," he said for the hundredth time, even though both knew the exact location, for they had measured it off with their footsteps on many an afternoon. He knew exactly how much material would be required to build their small house, one that would withstand the northeasterly winds and hold the warmth from the massive fireplace that he and Philippe would design.

"And the neighbors will help," Angelique reminded him.

The conversation was a litany between them, repeated every Sunday afternoon following the Sunday meal at the Boudreau home one hundred yards down the hill. But the image of their new home always brought a fresh burst of joy to their hearts and provided a sweet introduction for the deep kiss they hungrily shared. With a start of joy, Joseph realized that the cabin was already built, waiting for them, waiting for Sunday. . . .

He leaned forward, longing to inhale the lilacs that nestled in her hair, to brush his lips once more across the lips that were as soft and sweet as rose petals. But she was withdrawing from him, the expression on her face changing from one of sheer beauty to one from which all blood had drained. And now those lips were trembling his name in a strident plea. Joseph!

He moved, trying to get to her, but instead he felt the unforgiving iron frame of the cot that cramped his long legs. Slowly, ever so slowly, like one trying to return to reality, his head rolled on the pillow, and he felt a warm dampness against his cheek.

His thick lashes parted. Through a slit in his lids, he saw the low ugly ceiling and heard the heart-wrenching moans of other men. Awkwardly, he lifted a hand to his face, relieved that the fever had broken. He could feel a rough place here and there along his broad jawline, but this was of little concern to him. The fever had broken; he would live.

For another moment, he rubbed his matted eyes and ever so slowly his dazed mind struggled miserably back from the special place he had just shared with Angelique. He was back in the overcrowded sickroom on the ship. They had dropped anchor at the first port in the colony of Maine. The British had gone ashore to be treated, leaving the Acadians to suffer.

"You will stay here," an officer barked at Joseph, bringing him fully to his senses. He stared up at the man's dark shape in the doorway, then pushed himself up to the edge of the cot.

"This ship will be moving on, and if we need strong arms, you have proven your worth." The officer's head turned toward Philippe, and Joseph saw his face harden.

"He will not bother anyone," Joseph said quickly, glancing with concern at Philippe, who lay very still beside him.

"He can stay if you agree to dump him over when he draws the last breath."

Joseph nodded solemnly, trying to keep the hatred from showing in his eyes. To conceal this, he pushed himself slowly to his feet and ran a hand through his hair. "Is there anything you want done?" he asked, trying to sound humble, knowing he and Philippe would be better off going on with the ship.

He had overheard one of the men say the ship would dock in Boston Harbor. Madame Russo had a daughter who had married a Boston silversmith. Angelique had mentioned this to him once in conversation. If he could make contact with this daughter, it might be a way to keep in touch with Angelique—the best way, perhaps.

The officer was giving him more orders, and Joseph nodded, trying to pull strength from his weakened body. He had had only a light case of the pox. The hope of being reunited with Angelique had kept him alive, long after his sense of duty to Philippe had faded into his mind's feverish haze. Somehow, though, Philippe had managed to survive. Joseph said a silent prayer of gratitude. Now, he would do whatever was necessary to get them to Boston.

eight

Angelique prayed that Marie was resting peacefully as she and Claude approached the house. That hope was shattered, however, as soon as she opened the back door and heard her mother gasping for breath.

"Mother!" She rushed into the bedroom, then froze in the doorway.

Marie was writhing in pain, rolling back and forth, taking short, quick gulps of air.

"Mother, I am here." Angelique rushed to her side, removing the cloak and scarf and tossing them across the room.

"Thank God," her mother gasped. "Olga?"

"I know what to do," Angelique soothed her, hoping to convince herself as well as her mother. She could see, as she threw back the covers, that it was too late to send for anyone. The sheets were soaked with blood, and her mother was in hard labor.

Angelique glanced over her shoulder. "Claude, go and get towels, and then put the teakettle on for hot water."

Her mother gasped and heaved and clutched her stomach. "The baby. . .will come. . .soon." Her face contorted with pain.

Angelique rushed to the kitchen, where Claude was working with the teakettle. She saw he already had located some clean towels and had stacked them on the counter. "You will need thread," he was saying. "And something to clip the cord."

"How do you know this?" She looked at him in amazement.

"I am the middle one of three children. I had to assist the midwife the last time with my little sister, when Father was away."

"Oh," Angelique murmured, staring at him. God had sent her a helper after all, in the form of a ten-year-old boy with a calm, steady hand and a mind filled with wisdom. "Claude, thank you for being here. Thank you so much," she said, her voice choked.

"Do not fear." He turned clear blue eyes to her. "I will help you."

She nodded and hurried back to the bedroom. The sight of her mother in such pain unnerved her completely. "God, help us," she murmured as she reached her mother's side.

Claude had followed with a pan of hot water and the stack of towels. Angelique whirled toward the nightstand, where the candle flickered dimly. "Find another candle and light it," she called to Claude.

"You should wash your hands," Claude said, standing by patiently with a wet towel.

"Yes, of course."

"And where is your mother's sewing basket?"

Angelique tried to think, but her mind refused to move as she methodically washed her hands, flinching with each cry of pain that came from her mother's parched lips. She shook her head, unable to remember where the basket was.

Grabbing the towels, she placed them under her mother's abdomen. Her mother cried out and thrashed back and forth.

"You must try and be still," Angelique said, instinctively knowing that she must brace her mother's bent knees. She slipped onto the foot of the bed, holding her mother's knees firmly against her own quivering body.

Marie seemed to draw new strength from her weary body as she heaved again and again, crying out. At last, Angelique grabbed a towel to catch the small baby. *Something about it isn't right,* she thought foggily; *it looks shriveled and odd. And it isn't moving.*

Claude had found her mother's sewing basket, and now he was standing beside her with scissors and thread. "The midwife told me to push on the stomach—there is more that must come out," he said gently.

Angelique nodded mutely, wrapping the still baby in a towel. She barely heard what Claude had said, for the baby's tiny, lifeless body had struck her dumb. She let out a gasp of sorrow as she looked down at her new little brother. He was dead.

"Let me see the baby." Marie reached out for him, but Angelique hesitated.

"Mother. . ."

"What is it?" Marie's face was pale and drawn. It broke Angelique's heart to show her the little one, but Marie clutched persistently at her sleeve until she knew she had no choice. When the baby was in her mother's arms, she turned and fled from the room. She flung the back door open and went outside, her stomach heaving. The smoke from the village drifted up, making her heave once more, until she felt sicker than before.

"I am sorry," Claude spoke up from beside her, and she turned and stared through her tears at his kind little face.

"Thank you so much for helping," she sobbed. "I don't know what I would have done. . ."

"Your mother will be all right," he said, as though she needed encouragement.

"She is a very strong woman," Angelique agreed, wiping her wet face with the skirt of her dress. "But this. . ."

"Come back inside," Claude urged her, gently pulling at her arm.

She turned and followed him back into the kitchen and closed the door, more aware now of the acrid smell that seemed to fill the air. She must focus on her mother . . .and the baby.

She whirled to Claude, now her source of strength. "We will have to bury the baby," she whispered, horrified at the thought.

He nodded. "Can you find a good strong box? We can fill it with towels and—"

"Blankets. The blankets Mother knitted—" Angelique bit her lip, forcing herself to think. A strong box.

Suddenly, she recalled the beautiful square box Joseph had carved for her. Polished and gleaming, it decorated the center of her dresser. A treasure box, he had called it when he presented it to her on her birthday. It was large enough to store the special treasures from their walks together—seashells, dried wildflowers, a carved cross—yet it was not too large for the baby. In fact, it would be perfect.

She moved in a daze to the dresser in her bedroom, trailing her finger over the smooth wooden box as she lifted the cover and began to remove her little treasures, laying them carefully on the dresser. It broke her heart to give up the box, for she felt she was losing something of Joseph.

But her parents had just given up their only son, and that thought made her ashamed of herself for holding onto the wooden box. Quickly, she hugged the empty box against her chest, leaving the sweet scent of dried wildflowers and the sea to envelop her baby brother. That and the blanket her mother had made him would wrap him safe and warm.

Claude appeared beside her and gently took the box. He seemed to understand everything without having to be told.

When she entered her mother's bedroom, her breath caught. The baby was wrapped in the new blanket, tucked in the crook of Marie's arm against her breast. Marie was fast asleep.

Claude moved toward the bed, his eyes urging Angelique to do what she must. Ever so gently, she removed the still bundle and placed it in the lovely box. And then she and Claude went out to the apple orchard to find the perfect grave site for her little brother.

nine

All day Joseph worked at Clark's Wharf in Boston, loading and unloading trunks of everything in the world, it seemed to him. From the West Indies came sugar, molasses, and fruit. England sent silk and thread for the women, tea and coffee, and special spices that came from the Far East. All day long, Joseph's strong arms lifted the cargo, then carried it into the warehouses to be stored. Down by the sea the November wind tore at his thin body, but he pushed himself to keep on.

Often he cast his eyes to the northeast, far up the ocean, and he thought of his homeland and his beloved Angelique. Someday he would go back; somehow, someday. *God, provide a way,* he silently begged as he continued his hard work.

His strength had won favor with the British, although he knew he was used as a slave. Still, he consoled himself with the fact that he was not in the prison where many other French Acadians had ended up until the British could determine how best to use them. Joseph had even managed to persuade the British to allow Philippe, weak and useless to them, to remain with him in a drafty back room of the warehouse.

Their new home was poor and bare. They had only two cots, one candlestick, and some empty, upturned crates that served as tables and chests for the few items they still possessed.

Ship watchers guarded the ships, day and night, so there was no hope for the escape that in the beginning had been his plan. And there had not been a chance to search out silversmith shops for Madame Russo's son-in-law. He was too exhausted at night to do anything more than creep back to his room, where Philippe tried to have a paltry meal prepared for them.

As weary as he was, however, at night as Joseph lay on his bed, staring into the darkness, he was unable to sleep. He lay awake, listening to the ocean slapping around the piers, thinking of Angelique. As the weary hours slipped by, at last he would force his thoughts into prayer, and then at last a measure of peace would come to him. He never stopped praying that he and Philippe could go home to the women and the land they loved.

❧

God was listening to his prayers.

A few days later, a huge ship docked in Boston Harbor, and Joseph noticed an unusual crowd at the docks. It was not uncommon for people to gather whenever a ship came into port, for everyone was curious to see what was being unloaded from around the world, but this crowd was bigger than ever. Scanning the crowd, as usual Joseph did not see a single familiar face. With a sigh, he turned back to his work.

He had just placed a huge trunk on the deck, when to his astonishment, Philippe slipped quietly to his side and tugged at his sleeve. Joseph stared at him, startled that Philippe would dare come to the harbor. Philippe must be curious about the crowd, Joseph reasoned; perhaps he hoped to spot someone he had once known in his old life. Automatically, Joseph's eyes scanned the people around them, hoping that none of them would prove to be a danger to Philippe.

"He is in the crowd," Philippe muttered under his breath. Joseph glanced at Philippe and noted a radiance in his face that had not been there since they had left Grand Pre.

"He will help us," Philippe whispered. An officer came near the line of men unloading the cargo, and Philippe darted back among the workers and disappeared.

Joseph's eyes scanned the crowd again, but he still saw only strangers. Pondering Philippe's words, he reached down for another trunk. Then realization struck and the trunk was suddenly feather light. Philippe had found Madame Russo's son-in-law. The silversmith!

ten

Angelique took the small nativity scene from its box on the top of the shelf, but she left all their other handmade Christmas decorations there. She and her mother had agreed they would honor the birth of Jesus, but they would have no other celebration. Quietly, Angelique handed the nativity scene to her mother. Then she went to the window and stood staring out, blinking back her tears.

When she turned around at last, Marie sat at the kitchen table, dusting the tiny manger that Joseph had made for them last year. Angelique looked away. She could not bear to see his work, for it brought memories of the Christmas before. Instead, she went to the fireplace and sat down in her father's chair, staring into the low fire.

They had to wear warm clothing now and keep only a small fire going to conserve the coals left in their tin bucket. They had been out of wood for a week, but Madame Russo had sent her grandson over with coals, warning them to keep a live coal always burning.

Tears blurred the small flickering flame. Shivering, Angelique nestled deep in the heavy shawl her mother had knitted, but she was barely aware of the cold. She did not feel anything, only sadness, a terrible sadness.

Early one morning, just at daybreak, she had walked in the meadow past the new house where by now she should have been living with Joseph. She had fallen to the ground, clutching the cold dirt, sobbing for what had been taken from them—their home, their love.

Except for that one morning, she had not dared leave the house for over a month now, for fear that she would see the officer who had so boldly tossed her into his carriage and brought her home. Nightly, she and her mother prayed that no one would bother them, and so far, they had not. They did not want to be sent away from their home, not yet, not until they could find out where Joseph and Philippe had been sent.

Grand Pre had fallen into an uneasy calm. No more buildings had been burned, and Claude reported that no one else had been killed. The remaining villagers, he said, scuttled around the streets with their heads down, fearful of angering the Redcoats that stood guard on every corner.

"Angelique?" her mother called, rousing her from her thoughts.

"Mmm?" The Sunday church bells peeled softly, and Angelique drew a deep breath, rolling her head on the chair to peer back at her mother.

Marie had picked up the Bible and was flipping through the soft worn pages. "Christmas is coming," she said softly. "We should be preparing our hearts for the Lord's birth. On this Sunday morning, I want to read the nativity story. We need to remember to look beyond the sadness of our own lives."

"We've read that story every day this week," Angelique snapped, then bit her tongue and stood up. "I'm sorry. I'm feeling sorry for myself when I should be feeling sorry for you. You've been brave and strong."

She walked over and sank down at the table beside her mother. Marie had put the nativity scene on a small stand, and Angelique was grateful not to have to look at Joseph's manger again.

"God's Word is all that keeps me going," her mother said. "We must believe His promise that He will be with us; He will not fail or forsake us. Although our situation looks grim, we must not give up hope." Marie reached across the table and touched her daughter's hand. "Remember; you promised Joseph."

Angelique lowered her head, dashing a hand up to wipe away the tears she could no longer hold back.

Her mother wrapped her fingers around Angelique's. "God is providing for Philippe and Joseph, just as He is for us. I know that; I believe that, and you must as well."

Angelique nodded, staring at her mother's thin pale hand, the long fingers that had given so much comfort to so many. "Yes, I will try harder," Angelique said, her voice trembling.

She sat silent, staring at the Bible. Her mother sighed and turned the pages from Luke to the Old Testament. "Since we have been reading the story of Christ's birth, I will go back to our favorite psalm for a change. I always find great comfort in it, no matter how many times I read it."

Angelique nodded and listened while her mother read the familiar words from the Twenty-third Psalm.

"The LORD is my shepherd; I shall not want. He maketh me to lie down in green pastures: he leadeth me beside the still waters. He restoreth my soul: he leadeth me in the paths of righteousness for his name's sake. Yea, though I walk through the valley of the shadow of death, I will fear no evil: for thou art with me; thy rod and thy staff they comfort me. Thou preparest a table before me in the presence of mine enemies: thou anointest my head with oil; my cup runneth over. Surely goodness and mercy shall follow me all the days of my life: and I will dwell in the house of the LORD for ever."

Angelique sat very still as her mother finished, for she was considering each word that had been read. The words she had heard so many times spoke to her in a new way. Would God really prepare a table for them, she wondered, here, now, when they were surrounded by their enemies? Was God's goodness and mercy following them, even though they could not see?

Angelique thought of the small, empty house in the meadow where she had hoped to live with Joseph. Her heart ached to think of the empty rooms, silent and cold, waiting for them. Would they ever live together in that house?

She didn't know the answer to her question. But in the meantime, could she rest in the assurance that she was living in God's house, no matter what happened, all the days of her life?

A light rap sounded on their door. Claude always knocked gently, and Angelique got up from the table and hurried across to the door to unbolt it. She reached out to hug the boy, but the embrace was a quick one, for his face was flushed with excitement.

"Father is here!" he said, jerking his tam from his head so quickly that his brown hair tumbled onto his forehead.

"Your father? Here?" Angelique gasped. She had almost given up hope that Claude's father would be able to get into Grand Pre.

"He has come for you," Marie spoke up. "That is wonderful, Claude."

"Wonderful for you, too! He just arrived by boat and he has news for you." The boy's dark eyes glowed as he looked from Angelique to Marie. "Mr. Landry and Mr. Boudreau are in Boston. We are to bring the two of you back with us."

Marie gasped and stared at Claude as though unable to believe her ears. But Angelique had heard every word and now she was hugging Claude again. They laughed out loud together, and then she began to cry.

"Oh, Claude, when can we speak to your father? And how does he plan to get us out of Grand Pre? And what about your grandmother?" The questions tumbled from her lips between sobs of joy.

"He can come over now. He asked me to see if it is convenient."

"Of course it is convenient." Marie had come to her feet now, and tears of joy were glowing in her eyes as well.

Claude nodded, then turned to Angelique. "Oh, I almost forgot. My grandmother wishes to speak with you."

"With me?"

"Yes." His face darkened. "She is not going with us. She will not leave her home. She says she is too old to travel so far."

"Who will care for her?" Marie asked.

Claude's shoulders drooped, and Angelique could see

this brave young boy was going to find it difficult to leave his grandmother.

"We will find someone in the village to care for her, Claude. Do not worry," Angelique reassured him.

"Father will do that. First, he wants to speak with you."

"We will be waiting," Marie said. "I will make tea."

Claude shook his head. "He will not stay that long. He is very. . ." He seemed to be searching for a word. "Very businesslike."

Angelique nodded, sensing that Claude was not close to his father. She touched his shoulder again. "You will get to see your mother and your brother and sister."

His eyes brightened at those words, and he nodded. "I must go."

He was out the door, moving with his usual lightning speed, and Angelique whirled to face her mother, her fingers pressed against her cheeks. They were warm, and she knew that for the first time in weeks her face was rose-colored again.

"Mother. . .can you believe it? Is it possible. . .?"

Her mother was smiling, wiping away her tears. "All things are possible for those who believe. We must make a list of what to take. And we will do whatever is required." She clasped her hands together and said quietly, "Thank You, dear Lord, for keeping our loved ones safe. Please deliver us safely to them now."

❧

Spencer Wolfe, Claude's father, was a small, intense man who clearly had no time to waste. As soon as Angelique opened the door, he entered quickly and headed straight for the table where Marie sat.

"Madam." He inclined his head. "I have seen your husband in Boston."

Marie clutched her breast and gasped. "You have seen Philippe? He is well?"

He hesitated. "Yes." He looked across at Angelique. "He and Joseph are working at Clark's Wharf there. They have asked me to bring you back with me, since I have come for Claude, but there can be no delay. We must take the first ship out in the morning. It departs at nine. I hope you can be ready to leave by then."

Angelique and Marie stared at one another in silence for a few seconds. They could have been ready to leave immediately if they had to. They would do whatever they needed to do to be reunited with their men. Silently, they nodded their heads.

"Right," Mr. Wolfe said. "As of now, I have permission for the two of you to return with Claude and me. But we must go quickly. Take only one trunk with you." He paused, his eyes sweeping over the house. "I can make no promises about the house or anything else. I cannot guarantee that your remaining possessions will be safe. You understand?"

"You have done enough," Marie said calmly. "We will be ready to depart by eight bells—is that soon enough?"

He nodded. "Claude and I will come for you then. I am going back to the village to complete the arrangements. And Madame Russo would like to speak with you," he said to Angelique as he turned for the door.

"I'll get my cloak and go now," she answered quickly.

The man was gone in the same haste with which he had arrived. Angelique ran to her mother, squealing with delight. "Oh, Mother, can you believe it?"

Marie, though much more composed then, hugged Angelique hard. "God is bringing us back together. We will do exactly as Monsieur Wolfe says. Now, rush over and see to Madame Russo."

Angelique's heart raced wildly as she half-trotted through the fields to the home of Madame Russo. It was not her quick steps that made her heart pound, though, but her new joy.

Monsieur Wolfe's attitude was less friendly than she had hoped, but she understood that he was taking a risk for them; she and her mother would do whatever he said. And she would take good care of Claude on board. Angelique suspected that this was why Madame Russo wanted to see her.

Claude had been watching for her, and the door flew open before she reached the doorstep.

"Claude, I am so happy," Angelique burst out, giving him a hug.

There was a mixture of excitement and hesitation on his face, and she assumed that he was concerned for his grandmother. She was removing her cloak as she walked quickly to the bedroom. There she found Madame Russo lying very still, staring at the ceiling.

"Madame Russo, it is Angelique." She gripped the old woman's bony fingers.

Madame Russo's head turned on the pillow, and she tried to smile, although her eyes were as glazed as before. "Thank you for coming. Would you ask Claude to come in here, please?"

Angelique turned and saw that Claude was already

standing in the door. "I am here, Grandmere."

"You are to stay in this young woman's care until you reach your mother. Is that understood?"

Claude's little face was grave. "Yes, it is."

"Now please go out in the backyard and see if there are any apples left. I want to send something to Marie."

"Oh, that isn't—" Angelique began.

"Yes," Madame Russo interrupted sharply.

Claude's light steps flew through the house and out the back door as Madame Russo motioned Angelique closer.

"Where is Mr. Wolfe?" she whispered.

"He has gone to the village," Angelique answered.

"Good." The old woman let out a sigh of relief. "Now listen to me. I do not trust him. I did not want my daughter to marry him." Tears rose in her eyes. "But she chose to do so, and she will not return to Grand Pre."

"Are you saying we won't be safe with him?" Angelique asked, horrified by the thought that they would not be able to go after all.

Madame Russo heaved a deep sigh that seemed to shake the length of her thin body beneath the quilt. "No; I think you will be safe. Because of Claude, he will see you there safely. But, please, on the journey, I ask you to love and care for Claude. His father is. . .abrupt."

Angelique nodded. "Please do not worry about Claude. I will care for him as though he were my own little brother. In some ways, he is like that to me."

Madame Russo gave a nod of satisfaction, but her face was paler now. "Tell Marie I am sorry about the babe. But I must speak quickly. Underneath my bed is a chest of fine silver, forks, knives, and spoons. It is quite valuable. Get it."

Angelique dropped to the floor and fumbled over house shoes and discarded handkerchiefs, finding nothing at first. Then, far back under the bed, she touched a box. Stretching her arm as far as she could reach, she was able to pull it out. The box was a small one, covered with dust, and it had obviously been underneath the bed for a very long time.

"What do you want me to do with this?" Angelique asked.

"Tell no one," the old woman said quickly. "Take it back home with you and hide it well. Claude wants to return here someday. You can use it to buy property for your family and for Claude."

But could they ever return? With a sigh, Angelique realized that Claude, half British, would be able to do so, even if she and her family would not.

"You want me to hide it on my property?" she asked.

"Yes. Claude said you buried the baby. Put the chest of silver in the grave and cover the dirt back as it was. Do this tonight. After dark." The back door slammed, and the old woman jumped. "This is our secret," she whispered just before Claude reappeared.

Angelique realized this woman did not even want her grandson to know about the silver—not yet, so she quickly spread her skirt over the box as Claude went to his grandmother's side.

"Grandmere, the apples are frozen and brown. There is nothing out there that looks worthy of. . ."

"It is all right, Claude. I have reassured your grand-

mother that all we want is to see her cared for and safe."
Angelique turned back to Madame Russo. "Who should I go and contact? Is there someone you would like to care for you when we are gone?"

The old woman's body stiffened. "Claude's father has gone to employ a nurse for me. Here now, give me a hug and go. Claude, go stoke up the fire, please."

Claude disappeared again, and Angelique bent over Madame Russo, pressing her cheek to the woman's gray skin. "You can trust me," she whispered.

"There are potatoes in the kitchen," Madame Russo spoke up, squeezing her hand. "Get a cloth and wrap up some to take home." She spoke loudly, and Angelique realized this was for Claude's benefit.

"I will wrap the box in the cloth with the potatoes," she whispered, and the woman nodded.

"Now you must hurry back and prepare to leave on the morrow." Madame Russo spoke sharply now, as though she were forcing herself to be strong for everyone.

"Yes. We will pray for you." Angelique bit her lip, aware that she would probably never see this woman again.

"I will be fine," Madame Russo said. Her eyes drifted back toward the ceiling, closing Angelique out.

Unable to speak, Angelique turned and hurried into the kitchen while Claude knelt at the fireplace, using the poker to stoke up the coals. She snatched up a few potatoes, then grabbed the first cloth she spotted and wrapped it around the box as she reached for her cloak.

"I am going now, Claude," she called. "I will see you in the morning. Your grandmother is sending potatoes instead of the apples." She stood in the doorway and held up the tightly wrapped treasure.

❧

Late that evening, after her mother had gone to bed, Angelique took the silver chest, still wrapped in the cloth, and placed it in a dishpan with two large wooden spoons. Silently, she slipped out the back door. The night was cold and clear, lit by a full moon.

Quickly, she made her way to the grave of her little brother. The ground was still freshly dug, and the dirt was soft, easy to scoop out with the wooden spoons. She placed all the loose dirt in the dishpan, and although the task took her over an hour, when she was done, she felt a sense of accomplishment that she had managed the job on her own. And she had told no one, not even her mother. Her loyalty to Madame Russo was complete.

Besides, the news of the silver would not comfort her mother. Angelique doubted they would ever return to their homeland—but Claude would come back. And someday, when the time was right, she would tell Claude about his inheritance.

eleven

"Joseph, we must leave," Philippe whispered over the warmed-up potato stew that neither was able to touch. "I received word today that one of the officers saw me talking with Spencer Wolfe. He has been watching you and me ever since. We must go to another part of town, somehow. Then I will send word to Monsieur Wolfe upon their return. We cannot be connected to him or it will be dangerous for all of us."

Joseph nodded, his mind racing furiously. "Will they suspect anything when he returns from Grand Pre with two women?"

"They will search the ship; they always do. He plans to tell the authorities upon his return that he has brought back a cook and a governess for his children. But they cannot know we are connected. He is very nervous about this."

Joseph nodded, comprehending the risk Monsieur Wolfe was taking. "If only he can bring back Angelique and Madame Boudreau. . . ."

"He will do that because his wife insists."

A cold wind rattled the tin roof of the warehouse, and the men automatically leaned closer to the tiny fire.

"I will get a night job," Joseph said. "They will be less likely to find me if I am working at night."

"And we should go to the opposite side of town.

Monsieur Wolfe lives near Government Street. If you can obtain work there. . ."

"I can," Joseph said firmly, lifting his eyes to Philippe as new strength flowed through his body. "If he will bring Angelique to me, I will do anything!"

twelve

The voyage was a nightmare. Angelique and Marie had been given the tiniest compartment on the ship, and Monsieur Wolfe had ordered them to be seen as little as possible.

Staying in their compartment was no problem for Marie, for the agonies of seasickness kept her in her bed. She had not been prepared to suffer like this. Luckily, however, mal de mer was not so very different from morning sickness, and she still had raspberry leaves and dried berries tucked in the tiny navy cloth pouch pinned to her waistband. The pouch also contained her wedding band, the locket Philippe had given her, and a tiny gold baby ring that Angelique had worn as a baby.

As it happened, the raspberry tea transformed violent nausea to a gruesome yet tolerable experience for Marie. She was just sick enough that Monsieur Wolfe had no worries about Marie being seen strolling on deck. She dared not venture from the wood-slab cot with its doubled blanket of horsehair that served as a mattress; she was too afraid of losing the small amount of broth Angelique had obtained for them to eat.

Claude, looking crestfallen and guilty, had brought them some boiled eggs, a loaf of bread, and once a smoke-stained kettle of tea wrapped in a thick towel. They did not ask where he had obtained any of these precious items, but he knew they were grateful.

"Soon you will see your family." Angelique offered the sad little face the only words of cheer that occurred to her.

A look of relief passed quickly over his features. "Yes. And you, too."

On his last visit, he had turned to leave, then stopped and stood staring at the door, his narrow back tensed.

"What is it?" Angelique asked gently, sensing that he was upset.

"I am sorry that Father is so mean to you. It is his way."

She knelt beside him and reached for his hand, entwining her fingers with his. "Claude, your father is risking his life to help us. We are deeply appreciative. I do not think he is mean."

But although she tried to feel only gratitude for Monsieur Wolfe, she could not help but think he was a cold man. He was abrupt and unaffectionate with his own son, and Angelique had already come to understand why Claude's grandmother did not trust Spencer Wolfe.

"He is not that way with my mother," Claude said, offering one redeeming feature about the man.

"He is good to your mother? I am glad," Angelique replied.

Claude nodded, but his shoulders slumped a bit, as though someone had invisibly placed a heavy load on his back again.

"Tell me about your father's silversmith shop," Angelique said, trying to change the subject so that Claude would not look so dreary.

He drew a ragged little breath. "He makes teapots,

many of them, and jewelry, candlesticks, even shoe buckles."

"That sounds interesting," Angelique said, trying to encourage him to talk more about the silversmith business.

Claude lifted his head and gazed into space. "I have no interest in becoming an apprentice to his trade. I want to return to Grand Pre and be a seaman like my grandfather."

Angelique patted his shoulder, thinking of the silver she had buried for him. "I'm sure you will be able to do that, Claude. Now, smile for me."

For the first time, a little smile appeared on his face, bringing light to his sad eyes.

"Everything will be all right," she assured him as she got to her feet. He nodded hopefully, then turned to leave.

After he closed the door, Marie, who had appeared to be asleep, spoke up. "His mother was a beautiful young thing, but she was always so bored with Grand Pre." Marie's voice was slow and weak, half muffled by the shawl that served her as a pillow. "Dominique wanted the excitement of a city, and when she was sixteen and Spencer Wolfe was—at least thirty, I'd say—he came to Grand Pre on business. As soon as he spotted Dominique in one of the shops, he was determined to take her back with him." Marie sighed heavily. "And that silly girl was just as determined to marry a well-to-do merchant from Boston."

Angelique sat down on the wood-slab bed, wondering why anyone would want to leave her beloved homeland. "Funny," she mused, staring at the dull gray wall, "I never had a desire to go to Boston, but here we go." She tried to fill her voice with a lighthearted note.

❧

Their relief upon their arrival in Boston was quickly mixed with frustration and uncertainty. As they were rushed from the ship's walkway into a mass of strangers, they were greeted by a bitter gray morning. Spencer Wolfe marched on ahead of them, having cleared them with the officials as maid and governess for his wife.

He then dashed off, offering no help with their trunk. When Claude stopped to assist them, his father impatiently yanked Claude by the sleeve, and now the boy raced to keep up, tossing tormented glances over his shoulder.

Claude finally broke free of his father's grasp and turned back to Angelique and Marie. The crowd swept over him like a tidal wave, as he fell, struggled up, and fell again, trying to reach them in the crushing onslaught of people who were all eager to get their feet on solid land. At last, he reached them, and he had managed to relieve Marie of he half of the trunk and was assisting Angelique, when his father's sharp voice broke through the mist.

"Claude! Let go. Brutus will help."

Gasping for breath, Angelique peered over the heads and shoulders in front of her. Beyond the crowd, she spotted all sorts of wagons, buggies, and even some elegant carriages.

The man Mr. Wolfe had yelled for strode into the crowd. He was a swarthy hulk of a man who looked as though he should be wearing a black patch over his heavily lidded eyes. He fetched the trunk with one hand, while tossing a cursory glance over Angelique. He ignored Claude and Marie completely.

Saying nothing, he lunged ahead, clearing a path for them. The snips and crude remarks hurled at little Claude when he had braved the crowd were not risked on Brutus.

The carriage they finally reached was so lush and comfortable that Angelique and Marie paid no attention to Mr. Wolfe's cold silence. When Brutus cracked the whip again, jostling the carriage over the cobblestones, Marie cleared her throat and ventured a question.

"Where are we to meet Philippe and Joseph?"

"I don't know," Wolfe answered flatly. "I agreed to bring you to my house, but they are not to come there. I assume a messenger will be sent to tell us of their whereabouts. They have left the wharf and gone into hiding."

Angelique and Marie exchanged startled glances. At least Philippe and Joseph were here, and they would find them, sooner or later. Angelique gripped her mother's hand and squeezed the gloved fingers softly. Her heart was soaring with happiness by the time they reached the elegant townhouse on Government Street.

Her hopes fell into a bottomless pit, however, with the news that greeted them. A distraught maid met them at the door and looked gravely at her employer.

"Mr. Wolfe, I have terrible news."

"What is it?" he stormed at her.

Her eyes swept past him to the two strange women, then landed on Claude, and she hesitated. "Please come in."

They entered the marble hallway, Brutus bearing the

trunk on his shoulder, while Claude had suddenly become very nervous, looking anxiously toward the closed doors.

"Where are Lucie and George?" he asked quickly. "And my mother?"

There was an awkward moment of silence, during which Angelique caught her breath. The house was too still, too quiet. She knew the frightened little maid was deathly serious.

"Speak, woman. Is your tongue tied?" Wolfe demanded. "Where is everyone?"

"We tried to reach you—"

"I haven't time for your dawdling." He pushed her aside and started for the stairs.

"Wait, please, Mr. Wolfe." The maid caught up with him, tears flowing down her cheeks now. "There has been an outbreak of the pox. The children are quite ill; your wife. . ." She was clearly unable to finish the sentence, but he gave her no time. He was flying up the stairs, taking them two at a time, his boots crashing against the marble.

Claude rushed to the maid's side, seizing her arm. "Tell me what has happened."

"Oh, dear Claude," she said, sobbing now.

"Tell me," Claude urged, looking pale and frightened. He squared his shoulders, obviously dreading the truth.

"Your mother. . .she. . .passed away last evening."

And then they heard the guttural moan wrung from a man with a broken heart. A loud wild sound followed, then heavy wracking sobs.

"He has already found her," the maid sighed, dabbing at her eyes.

Claude was running up the steps now, his thin body moving frantically upward toward the tragic scene he was about to witness.

Marie was the only one able to speak. She touched the maid's hand gently. "Madame Wolfe died?" she asked reverently.

The maid nodded, sobbing. "It hit her hard, sudden. George ran for the doctor, but her fever had already gone so high." She sobbed into her handkerchief. "Her heart just stopped beating."

Mixed with the awful guttural moans, they heard now a young cry, the pitiful sound of Claude's broken heart. Angelique took a step forward, wanting to go to him, to hold him in her arms. But the maid stopped her.

"Mr. Wolfe will not permit anyone outside the family up there now. There are nurses with the children. They are not quite as ill as their mother was, but we don't know. . ." Her voice drifted off like a ship lost in a fog.

"We will help with the children," Marie said, her own voice quiet and determined. "I have had experience with the fever. Please allow us to go to the children and see if we may relieve the nurses."

The maid hesitated, then relented, obviously not sure what she should do. "The first two doors on the right," she called after them as they mounted the stairs.

They found the sick children with the half-asleep nurses, who were clearly exhausted. The little girl had brown hair and small features. In the pine four-poster bed, beneath the soft woolen blankets, she looked very pale. She was either asleep or in a coma.

"She is not quite as bad as the boy. The oldest son," the nurse said, pulling herself wearily from her bedside chair to place another cold cloth on the little girl's forehead. "He. . .the doctor. . .doesn't know if George will live."

Marie had already turned and was hurrying to the next room. Angelique lingered by the bed, touching the small delicate hand gently.

"When did she get sick?" Angelique asked softly.

"The maid said a man came here to leave a message. His face was scarred from the pox. We think he brought the sickness." The nurse glanced at Angelique and frowned. "He spoke as you do. With a French accent."

Angelique's heart froze. *Please, God. Don't let Philippe or Joseph be connected to this.* But she had a terrible feeling, one she couldn't quite pinpoint; it was the same feeling of dread that all the women of Grand Pre felt when one of their men's ships did not return on time—and then never returned.

She turned from the bed, scarcely taking notice of the nice room with its elegant furnishings, a room just perfect for the little girl, whom Claude had once told her was four years old. Angelique stepped into the carpeted hallway. The heavy sobs from down the hall were muffled now, yet the terrible sadness hung like a black cloud over the upstairs.

Gently, she turned the knob on the next door and stepped into a larger room, one with bookcases that held leather-bound books, various forms of artwork, and a miniature ship. She also saw several pieces of silver, objects to be treasured by a boy.

In the dim candle glow, she saw the nurse huddled over the bed. Marie stood on the opposite side, her face revealing the depth of her concern. Angelique tiptoed to the bedside and caught her breath. Despite the cold cloth the nurse pressed to his forehead, the boy's face was flaming red. His nightshirt was open, and Angelique could see the gleam of a salve rubbed onto his chest.

Her eyes turned to her mother beside her, and when Marie turned her face to her, she saw the fear rising in her eyes. "How long has he been this way?" Marie asked the nurse.

"He has grown worse the past hour. It is like his mother," the nurse whispered. "The fever is rising so high. . . ."

"Where is my trunk?" Marie whirled to Angelique, who merely stared blankly at her.

Marie didn't wait for Angelique's answer, but hurried out of the room. Angelique followed close behind her. *What is in our trunk,* she wondered, *that could possibly help this desperately ill boy?*

They were downstairs on their knees, plundering through the trunk Brutus had left in the hall, when Spencer Wolfe's voice raged out from the top stair.

"Your husband has done this!" he shouted at Marie. "Like a fool, he came here himself to deliver the message of their whereabouts. He bore signs of the pox, according to Brutus. He has killed my wife!"

The man was furious, and for a moment his black wrath held Marie and Angelique captive. But Marie, always levelheaded, chose to ignore his raging words. She lifted a small cloth bag, stood, and faced him.

"I have herbs here that we used on the island to break the fever. I would like to make a tea."

"Get out of this house. Both of you. It is because of you that this terrible thing has happened."

Angelique was struck dumb by his words; she had

never seen such anger and hate.

Marie quietly walked to the foot of the stairs and looked up at him. "Will you be so stubborn that you allow your son to die, as well? The nurse has admitted to us that he is getting worse. The leaves and tops of this herb have been successfully used to break the fever when children were all but dead. At least, let me try to save him. Obviously, no one else has."

Spencer Wolfe glared at her, but Claude, appearing out of the shadows, spoke up. "Please, Father. Allow her to help. Grandmere said all the Grand Pre women were wise in the use of herbs. She used them herself once to save Mother's life as a child. Mother told me the story."

Spencer Wolfe continued to glare at the two women, as though he could somehow use them to relieve the anger that turned his lips white and caused his body to tremble visibly beneath his thick cloak.

Marie quietly began to ascend the stairs. "I will do nothing without your nurse's permission," she said gently and somehow managed to ease past him. She rushed down the hall.

Angelique's mind raced. Hot water! She would need hot water to dissolve the roots and make a tea for the boy to drink.

The hysterical maid had reappeared, more composed now, although her eyes were red and swollen, and her cheeks were flushed.

"Where is the kitchen?" Angelique asked quietly.

The maid said nothing, but led the way down the corridor to a back room, a huge kitchen, where to her relief, Angelique spotted a kettle steaming on the hearth of the stone fireplace.

Saying nothing to the sturdy woman peeling potatoes at a counter, Angelique hurried over, grabbed a thick mitt, and removed the kettle. "A bowl and a cup," she said as she turned to the maid. The woman was watching her with a rather stupid expression, as though she was not quite sure what was going on. "We need a bowl and a cup for the nurses upstairs."

At the mention of the nurses, the big woman who had been peeling potatoes swung her woolen skirts around and reached into a cupboard. Producing a thick tin mug and bowl, she thrust them at Angelique. Angelique grasped them to her chest, while she awkwardly tried to keep the hot kettle a comfortable distance from her face.

Carefully, she ascended the steps, relieved to see that the raging Monsieur Wolfe was nowhere in sight. Nor was Claude. But as she passed the door of the boy's room, she could hear her mother and the nurse speaking in a low voice.

As she moved on to the next room, Angelique was trying to balance her load while opening the door, when Claude suddenly appeared, his little hand thrust out to turn the knob for her.

"Thank you," she whispered. As she entered the room, Claude reached out to relieve her of the steaming kettle.

Angelique went to the bedside of the little girl to relieve the other nurse, who was already dozing in the chair. Quietly, Angelique pulled a small stool up beside the bed and sat down. Glancing at the dozing nurse, she stood again and reached forward to touch the little girl's face. Her cheeks were warm but not as flushed as those of her brother. Perhaps if the herb broke the boy's fever, Monsieur Wolfe would be willing for it to be used on the little girl.

Suddenly, Angelique became aware that Claude was standing close behind her. She looked over her shoulder at him, taking in his swollen eyes and slumped shoulders. He motioned to her, and she followed him out of the room into the hall.

Tears filled his eyes. "You must leave. Father is furious. I have learned from the cook that the man who brought the message is working at a bakery not far from here." He looked quickly up and down the hall, his little body trembling.

Angelique followed his eyes and realized that he was terrified of his father. She could also see by his face that he was heartsick over all that had taken place.

"The cook just moved out of an apartment house only a few streets from here," he continued. "She says the rent is cheap."

Before Angelique could answer, she heard steps thundering up the stairs. She pushed Claude aside and rushed into the other bedroom. Her mother was holding the little boy's head while the nurse gently poured the tea into his mouth. Angelique quietly shut the door behind her. She had just opened her mouth to warn her mother that Monsieur Wolfe was apparently on his way, when the door flew open again.

"Get out! Now!" Wolfe shouted, apparently not concerned that he might wake the boy.

Marie did not look up. She continued to hold the boy's head steady until the last of the tea trickled into his mouth. Then she gently lowered his head and looked at the nurse. "Continue to give him the tea. There's plenty of the herb there—"

"Mother." With a glance at Wolfe's face, Angelique grabbed her by the arm. "We have to leave."

Marie nodded. "I heard him. Good luck." She smiled at the nurse, who looked from Marie to her employer and suddenly turned pale. She tried to step in front of the cup and the herbs on the bedside table, as though Wolfe had not already seen what they were doing.

Marie did not look toward Wolfe as she walked across the room, her chin high. "We will go," she said to Angelique and went proudly through the door, as though the man was not standing there with murder in his eyes.

Angelique followed, silently praying that they would be able to leave the house without being shot or the authorities being called. Claude had given her some valuable information; if she could just find Joseph and her father, everything would be all right.

Once they reached the downstairs, she told her mother to go on, that she would catch up. She had to speak with the cook.

"Do not tarry," Marie said with a heavy sigh. "I don't think I have ever seen such a cruel man."

Marie continued on toward the front door while Angelique rushed back to the kitchen. "Can you please give me the name of the apartment house where you stayed?" she asked quickly.

The fat woman looked up, startled, her double chin trembling. "Don't have a name. Go up to the end of this block, take a right, walk straight for three blocks, and make a turn. It's the third house down."

"Thank you." Angelique heard Wolfe shouting at Claude from the stairway, and she rushed for the back door.

"You are to have nothing to do with them!" the man was roaring at his son. Angelique slipped out the back door and quietly shut the door on his voice.

She hurried up the dark alleyway to the front of the house, where she found her mother was walking slowly down the street. They did not even have their trunk with them, but it didn't matter. Somehow they would get the trunk later.

When she caught up with her mother, she saw that the dignity that had sustained her mother through this humiliating ordeal had deserted her now. Marie's shoulders were slumped, and her head was bent.

"Mother." Angelique touched her arm gently.

Marie turned her head, and Angelique saw her tear-stained cheeks in the glow of the gas lamp. She linked her arm through her mother's arm. "I have great news," Angelique whispered, hoping to cheer her mother. "Claude told me how to find Father and Joseph."

Marie stopped walking. For a moment she stood perfectly still, and then she turned to stare at Angelique, her face pale with the shock of all that had taken place.

"Don't ever come back," Spencer Wolfe's voice boomed behind them, echoing into the night. Angelique glanced back to see him standing on the porch, his hands balled in fists at his waist. His anger seemed to have transformed him into a lunatic. "And I warn you—I will get even with the man who brought this disease to our household!"

The ominous threat was accompanied by the loud slam of the front door. The women glanced at each other and continued to walk. Angelique squeezed her mother's arm tighter as they made a turn at the block. As she followed the directions the cook had given her, she made an effort to dismiss Monsieur Wolfe from her thoughts. She began relating to her mother what she had been told.

"We have no money," Angelique suddenly interrupted herself, remembering the meager amount they had tucked away in the trunk.

"Yes, we do," Marie replied calmly. "I have gold in my pouch, and I will bargain with the landlady. Our gold is valuable."

More valuable to us than anyone else, Angelique thought, recalling the wedding band and baby ring. But her mother was right. The gold would buy them a place to stay for tonight. Tomorrow, she would begin her search of all the bakeries in the neighborhood.

Despite the dark winter night, they had no problem finding the apartment house; the problem was the size of the apartment and the fact that it was unfurnished. After Marie mentioned they were temporarily without furniture, the older woman chewed her lip and looked back up the hall, obviously turning the question over in her mind.

"I have one bed in number 1 that is not in use. We can move it down there, I suppose. There are two gentlemen in number 3; they could assist us."

"That will be fine," Marie quickly replied. "If we can use the bed for now, we can soon find other furnishings."

The landlady nodded and proceeded to lead them down to the end of the hall. The house had obviously once been a grand home, like its neighbors, but years of neglect had left the wallpaper stained, and all the doors could use a fresh coat of paint. The landlady paused before the dark door of number 7, inserted the key, and unlocked the door.

She hoisted her candlestick and led them inside. It was a small front room, with low ceilings and plain wooden floors; Angelique guessed that the adjoining bedroom had once been a large closet. They could have easily fit these tiny quarters in their comfortable living room in Grand Pre. *But we are not in Grand Pre,* she reminded herself. *We are in Boston. Joseph and Father are in Boston! Nothing else matters.*

"This will be just fine for us," Marie said, opening the precious pouch that contained their prized possessions. "Will you consider any of these as payment for our rent and the use of a bed and candlestick or two?"

The woman turned Angelique's baby ring over in her palm, admiring the soft glisten of gold, then checked the wedding band. "Yes, these will do," she said.

Angelique could hardly withhold the gasp that escaped her. The woman was robbing them!

Marie hesitated, glancing back toward the one window and the dark night outside. "Very well," she said at last. "How long will we be permitted to stay with these as our payment?"

The woman was holding the wedding band up to the candlelight, appreciating the gleam of old gold. "A month," she said, pocketing her new treasures. "I will get linens for you, and the bed and candlesticks."

Marie nodded. "Very well."

Angelique stared at her mother as the woman hurried out of the room. "Mother, she is robbing us blind," Angelique protested in a whisper.

"We have no choice." Marie leaned against the wall as though she were suddenly exhausted.

Angelique realized then that her mother had pushed

herself to the limits of her endurance. After all, only six weeks had gone by since the loss of her baby. And she was right, of course. They were homeless, cast out on the dark streets of Boston, dependent on strangers until they found Joseph and Philippe.

Angelique squeezed her mother's hand. "I pray that I will mature into a woman as brave and kind as you," she said, leaning forward to kiss her mother on the cheek.

Marie's pale face was transformed by a loving smile. "You are already that, my daughter. You are God's special blessing to us."

The sound of male voices mixed with the landlady's voice as the arrangements for the bed were made.

Angelique took a deep breath and started forming her questions for the landlady. The nearest bakeries? She would memorize each one, and she would look until she found Joseph. But she and her mother had already discussed this on ship. She must disguise herself, to be sure no one connected the two of them with a woman searching for two French Acadians.

She already knew how she was going to disguise herself. The only possession the cook had left behind in the room was a small potion of gray hair dye; it was exactly what she needed.

thirteen

Angelique waited until late afternoon to begin her search of the bakeries. She had paid the price of being noticed by British officers in Grand Pre, and even though her hair was gray and she dressed and walked like an old lady, she knew her search was dangerous.

During the day, the talk around the long table in the landlady's dining room, where the tenants gathered for meals, was of the French and Indian wars. The Indians were attacking the colonies, and although the people in Boston were outraged by this, Angelique had to bite her tongue to keep from asking who had owned the land first. Her sympathies, of course, were with the Indians, but Marie had already warned her to keep quiet, to show no emotion over whatever was discussed.

"What are you ladies doing here all alone?" one middle-aged gentleman with a thick handlebar mustache asked.

"We are waiting for my husband and my daughter's fiancé," Marie said smoothly. "They had business to attend to, and we are joining them here."

Angelique looked at her mother, amazed at how well prepared she was to supply an excuse for the protection of her family.

The talk then returned to the French and Indians, how atrocious they were in killing poor colonists, and soon Angelique excused herself and returned upstairs to prepare for her search for Joseph. Since they only had the clothes on their backs, she had chosen again to wear her mother's thick cloak. It would conceal her well, and sadly it was more threadbare than her own. She was determined to look the part of an older lady who was unwell and poor.

❧

Several hours later, she had lost count of the blocks she had walked. The darkness had come earlier than she expected, and she was filled with uneasiness. She had been to the three nearest bakeries the landlady had told her about, dawdling at each one, peering toward the kitchen, hoping Joseph would walk through the door. Lingering longer would have aroused suspicion, and she knew each time he was not there. She would feel his presence if he were; she would sense it. Their love was deep and true, and Angelique was certain that their souls were joined in a way that made their senses more aware each time the other was near.

At the last bakery, fighting tears of disappointment, she had admitted to the older woman behind the counter that she was searching for someone. Were there any other bakeries in the area?

The woman glanced out toward the darkened street as the town crier walked by, announcing the late hour. "There is one four blocks over. A small one. I think the owner only employs a couple of people." She leaned over the counter. "He's a penny-pincher miser."

Angelique forced a tiny smile and nodded. "Maybe I will look there."

The woman gave her the quickest route, then cautioned her to hurry. "You must pass a tavern, and it would not be wise to be out much later."

Angelique nodded. "Thank you. I will be careful."

fourteen

Angelique hobbled along the cobblestone street, feeling alone and out of place. The wind howled down from a black sky, snatching her dark skirts, nipping at the hood that protected her head. The hour was late; most of the shops were closing now. She peered up at the sign over the shop, then turned and entered the bakery. Could this be the one?

As soon as she entered, her heart gave a great leap. Behind the counter stood a sullen older gentleman—and beside him was Joseph.

Angelique ducked her head, struggling to hide her joy. Out of the corner of her eyes, though, she feasted on the sight of his black hair and dark eyes. As she closed the door behind, he turned toward her with a smile, showing his even white teeth against bronzed skin. Angelique's heart pounded within her chest.

Glancing at the owner, whose frown merely deepened at the prospect of one last customer after a twelve-hour day, Joseph stepped quickly to the counter.

"May I help you?" he asked. "Our special today is honey buns."

Angelique almost gasped out loud, for the sound of his familiar voice made her nearly burst with delight. She nodded, peering up at him from underneath her hood.

"I will get some for you," he said gently.

Does he really think he is speaking to an old woman?

Angelique wondered. Surely, he must know her, despite her disguise. She glanced nervously at the shop owner, knowing that she did not dare betray herself in front of this unfriendly man. Taking a deep breath, she forced herself to stand still and watch silently as Joseph quickly removed the crusty rolls from the brick oven, then wrapped them carefully in brown paper and tied the package with a length of string.

"One shilling," he said, darting a glance at the owner, whose sharp eye was on him. Something in Joseph's voice made Angelique's eyes fly to his, but then she quickly lowered her head once more, letting the hood shadow her face. She fumbled in her pocket and removed a worn lace handkerchief, then unknotted it carefully. Her last shilling dropped onto the counter.

"Thank you," the young man answered. "Do you have far to go on this cold night?" Angelique was certain she heard a tense tone in his voice, but this time she kept her head down, not daring to risk the shop owner's suspicions.

"Only to Government Street," she muttered in a low voice, then coughed. She wanted the baker to assume she was nothing more than a poor, sick old woman.

"Take care," Joseph called after her as she turned slowly, the warm buns in their brown cover gripped tightly against her chest. Angelique smiled to herself. She knew she had not mistaken the note of love in Joseph's voice. It was all she could do to keep herself from skipping as she went slowly down the street.

❧

"Lock up," the baker barked as he began to untie his apron.

Joseph hurried to the door, shoving the bolt. Then he stepped to the back room and removed his apron and cap and placed them inside the barrel of soiled linen. He removed his worn coat from the hook on the wall, and then he bid his employer good night and hurried out the door. Quickly, he circled to the front of the store, his heart beating fast, his hopes rising.

Down at the end of the block, he spotted the old woman, moving slowly along, and his steps quickened. Careful to keep his distance, he followed as she turned the corner onto Government Street. Passing the tavern, he looked through the smoked window and saw only a few patrons huddled at tables, oblivious to the street crowd.

The wind picked up, sending a shiver through his gaunt body. The soles of his boots were worn thin, and he had no gloves to protect his hands, but he thrust his fists into his pockets, too filled with joy to notice the cold.

The woman had reached a large house that was less affluent than its neighbors, a boardinghouse, no doubt. She clutched the rail and painstakingly climbed the steps that led to the front door.

Joseph closed the distance between them now; in a dozen steps he could easily reach her, but he restrained himself. He was waiting, waiting for the right time. His boots thudded over the cobblestones; surely she could hear him, but she did not turn around as she went through the door. He took the stairs, two at a time, reaching the front door before it closed behind her.

His eyes followed her down the narrow hallway that was lit with three candles on a small table, and his gaze skimmed each closed door along the hall, counting the tiny apartments, six of them. Hers was number 7, the last one at the end of the hall.

He heard the door to number 7 open, and he crept down the hall, reaching the door just before it closed. Pushing gently on the door, he slipped inside.

The room was furnished with upturned box crates as make-do furniture. Joseph smiled to himself, for the décor was much like that in the room he shared with Philippe. On one upturned crate was a candlestick, and the woman stood with her back to him, lighting a small candle. His breath caught in his throat, waiting for her to turn.

When she did, her brown eyes seemed to light the entire room. Her face was young and radiant; the pale lips curved quickly in a blissful smile.

"Joseph!" she cried as their eyes locked, and he managed to close the door behind him before he leapt forward. And then she was flying into his arms, toppling the hood back from her lovely face, radiant with joy.

"I thought I'd never find you," she said with a sob.

He gathered her thin body close, pressing his lips to her cold forehead. "Angelique, I never gave up," he said, as tears filled his eyes.

Her unblemished skin gleamed like polished ivory in the candle's glow. He reached for a strand of the thick hair and smiled into her wet brown eyes. "When we are old, I see that you will be as lovely as ever. Gray hair becomes you."

"The gray will wash out," she said, smiling, "but when I am gray again, I will still love you. And we will be together when we are old, we must believe that."

A woman cleared her throat from behind them. Joseph turned slowly and saw Angelique's mother. Marie looked thin and pale. "Madame Boudreau," he said gently as she came forward to embrace him.

He did not ask about the baby. Philippe had heard from Spencer Wolfe that she had lost the little one. Philippe had been anguished at the news and more eager than ever to be reunited with his wife.

"How is Philippe?" Marie asked, unable to hold back the tears.

"He is all right." He smiled gently. He couldn't bear to tell her that her husband was still recovering from the ravaging effects of the pox. "He is staying with me and I will return quickly with the good news—"

His words were interrupted by the sound of a door flung open below them. British voices lifted in command as the sound of fists pounding on doors reverberated through the building.

"The soldiers," Marie whispered, grabbing Joseph by the arm. "Quickly, you must hide."

He followed her into the tiny bedroom that held only a single bed with another upturned crate and a burning candle.

"Under the bed," Marie whispered.

Joseph dropped to the floor, flattening himself against the cold boards, attempting to fit his long body beneath the low bed.

Angelique's tears of joy quickly turned to tears of desperation, as the boots thudded to a halt beyond the thin wall and fists began to hammer on their door.

"No, God, please," she whispered, her fist pressed against her trembling lips. "Don't let them take him again!"

fifteen

To her horror, Angelique realized that her prayer was not going to be answered, for the room was suddenly filled with soldiers.

"Where is Joseph Landry?" one of the officers started demanding.

"Who?" Marie asked calmly, only to be ignored as they stormed through the rooms. One soon shouted his victory from the bedroom.

"Come out, you traitor!"

Angelique began to sob, her face in her hands, unable to bear the sight of the officers arresting Joseph. Marie came to her side, her arms around Angelique's heaving shoulders. Angelique lifted her tearstained face, knowing she must say something to Joseph, encourage him, promise him they would be together again.

But he was surrounded by soldiers who roughly pushed him forward and shoved a gun in his back. Joseph did not look over his shoulder at Angelique or Marie as they marched him out into the hall. One of the redcoated men turned back to them. "Your husband has already been arrested," he said, glaring at Marie. "Both men will be charged with treason. And you are not to leave the premises. You are under guard, as well."

"Where are you taking them?" Marie managed to ask.

"To jail, where they belong."

And then he slammed the door, leaving both Marie and Angelique in shock.

They were still frozen together, hugging one another, trying to comprehend what had taken place, when the door was thrown open again. The landlady marched in, her gray hair standing on end, her cheeks flushed.

"I expect you to be out of this house by morning," she shouted at them.

"They told us we are not to leave, that we are under guard," Angelique said between sobs.

The landlady thrust her hands on her ample hips and glared at both of them. "Do you realize how humiliating it is for me to have an officer standing on my porch, gun in hand? The other tenants may leave because of this. How dare you. . ."

"We will be leaving as soon as we are permitted to do so," Marie said evenly, looking the woman square in the eye. "It is not your fault that this has happened, but neither is it ours. We are French Acadians from Grand Pre, and the British soldiers hate all of us. But I have paid you well for our lodging; no one will think less of you when you tell them you had no idea who we were. We have done nothing to bother anyone here."

The woman said nothing, but the grudging expression on her face told them that she knew this was true. Without another word, she stormed out, slamming the door behind her.

Angelique rushed to the bedroom and collapsed on the bed, unable to stop the gulping sobs that racked her body. She felt as though her heart had just been broken in half. Seeing Joseph again, having her hopes rise to new heights, now made their separation even more unbearable. For one wild moment, she wished that she had clung to Joseph and maybe allowed the soldiers to shoot them both together. She was not certain she would want to live if they did anything to Joseph, and she felt she was already dying inside. *What will the Redcoats do to Joseph and Father?* she wondered desperately.

She felt the bed sink down beside her. Marie said nothing, but Angelique could hear her mother's soft sobs. For a long time, the women lay together, saying nothing, weeping as though there would never be any reason to hope again.

❧

They slept in their clothes. The night had seemed endless, and their sleep came in tortured naps, each trying not to disturb the other, even though they knew that they were both awake. What could they say? No words could soften the terrible ache inside their hearts, so neither bothered to speak.

Toward morning, Angelique felt Marie slip out of the bed, but she could not turn over and ask what she was planning to do. Angelique's heart was so heavy within her that she felt as though she could never get out of bed again. There was no reason to keep going now. All the hoping and dreaming and planning, the loss of the baby, the difficult voyage, the freezing search for Joseph, it had all drained her. She had no energy left to keep going now.

But as she lay there in the gray light, she knew she had to force herself to go on living. Somehow, that seemed to be what God asked of her. Still, that knowledge did not prompt her to get out of bed, to think of tea, or anything else. She merely lay still, exhausted from her weeping, drained of all hope, of all feeling.

Without Joseph, I might as well be dead, she thought dully, *because my life would only be an existence.* And what was the point? Why would God expect her to go on without Joseph?

The minutes slipped by, turned into hours, and the room grew bright with sunlight, but Angelique still did not stir from the bed. Sometime later that morning, she was conscious of voices in the living room, but she did not care. It was probably the landlady telling them to get out.

Then a familiar voice made her eyes open. It was a tender voice, one that she associated with a good heart. For a moment, she considered getting to her feet to see who was in the other room, but she decided she was only dreaming. No one in this cold world had a good heart; she and her family were trapped in a dark dungeon of despair.

Then Marie came to her bed and touched her arm. "Claude is here. You must get up and come hear what he has to say."

Angelique rolled over. "Claude?" But still she could not move; she could not force herself to get up, to make any effort toward conversation, even if it were with Claude. What did anything matter now?

But then the boy appeared in the doorway and she was forced to look at him.

"Your hair?" he blurted.

"Oh." Angelique had completely forgotten about the

gray. She touched a strand hanging onto her forehead and shrugged. "I dyed it hoping to disguise myself, but it didn't stop the soldiers from coming after Joseph."

He gripped his tam between his small hands, and beneath the windblown hair his face was pale and stark. Dark shadows underlined his eyes, and he seemed thinner than ever. It occurred to her that she should warn him about his health; he looked on the verge of being ill. And then she wondered if the sickness in his house had touched him as well.

He moved slowly toward the bed, his gentle brown eyes fixed on her with such compassion that Angelique tried to smile but failed. Tears gathered in his eyes as he sat down on the bed beside her. Saying nothing, he reached for her hand.

"I am so sorry. I will never forgive my father for what he has done."

It took a moment for Angelique to make the connection. "Your father? Ordering us out of the house? That is nothing compared to. . ." Her voice trailed away, and she turned her face toward the wall, trying not to cry anymore. She hadn't thought there could be any tears left, but there were.

"To arresting your father and Joseph?" Claude asked sharply. The outrage in his voice made Angelique peer up at him through her tears. He looked into her face, and then he squared his narrow shoulders. "My father is responsible for what happened, Angelique. He called the authorities after you left. The cook, the imbecile, told him where you were staying and that your fiancé was working at a bakery. After he left to come here last night, the British got his address from the man at the bakery. They went and arrested your father as well."

His words, though spoken with care and gentleness, drove the spear deeper into her heart. "If I had not overheard the entire conversation with the British officer, I would not have believed my father was capable of such cruelty," Claude continued. "He has become a monster. I hate him!"

Angelique sighed. She remembered thinking something about hatred back when they were still in Grand Pre; she remembered praying something. . . . Finally, she found her voice. "You must not hate, Claude," she said wearily. "Hatred will separate you from God—and how can we survive without God? Your father is in mourning for your mother, and his sorrow is coming out through rage. He has to be angry at someone for what has happened; someone must take the blame for his wife dying."

"But my sister is better, and even George's fever has broken. The doctor was there when I left. While he was talking with Father, I took the opportunity to slip out. But I did hear the doctor say that the herbs you gave George must have worked. My brother began to sweat soon after you left, and the sweating broke the fever."

"Yes," Marie spoke quietly from the door. "I have seen that happen before."

Claude turned and looked at her. "You saved my brother's life. In time, my father will come to understand that. If not, I will run away. I will not live with him."

"You must be grieving for your mother, too, Claude," Angelique said, remembering what a terrible shock and tragedy this had been for him as well. She sucked in a deep breath, realizing that her own pain had made her selfish.

Claude nodded, lowering his head as the tears trickled down his cheeks. "We will have the service this afternoon and she will be buried in the cemetery behind Christ Church." He looked with longing at Angelique. "I only wish you could be there. I do not care about any of the others who will be coming."

She squeezed his hand. "You must think about what your mother would want you to do, Claude. You must be brave for your brother and sister."

His little shoulders slumped forward inside his woolen coat. "I love my little sister, but George is just like my father. He cannot wait to become an apprentice and go into silversmithing. Naturally, this pleases my father." He paused as Marie handed him a handkerchief, and he wiped his wet face.

"Are your brother and sister aware of. . .what has happened? Your mother, I mean?" Angelique asked gently, feeling Claude's sadness and wanting to help him, however she could.

"My brother is still quite ill and doesn't quite understand what is going on. But Elizabeth knows and she is very sad. She is glad I am home. I will talk to her more later. I cannot believe, as Father does, that just because Monsieur Boudreau came to our back door, such terrible illness could have befallen our household. Some of the servants died as well. Perhaps one of them brought the illness to our home."

"Does the doctor think that Philippe brought the illness to your house?" Marie asked curiously.

Claude nodded sadly.

Marie shook her head. "I do not believe it happens that way. The pox doesn't occur overnight. It usually takes days before the pox appear, and from what I have gathered, this sickness came immediately after Philippe was there."

"That is what Cook said. I do not know."

"Well, for now we must think of the service for your mother. We are so terribly sorry." Marie looked at Angelique and spoke her thoughts aloud. "What about Madame Russo? Should we send word?"

Claude quickly shook his head. "All that keeps Grandmere alive is the hope of seeing Mother and me again. I cannot take that hope from her. It is better for her not to know. She may not live long anyway. . . ." His voice broke again.

"Whatever you think." Angelique nodded. "I think you are right. That is the wisest thing to do."

He whirled to look at her. "I am going back to Grand Pre as soon as I am able to leave. I do not like Boston; I want to go back there and live near the sea, to be a part of the life there."

"Yes, Claude, we understand," Marie spoke up. "But you must wait until there is peace there. This is not the time to return."

Will there ever be a time to return? Angelique silently wondered. She thought of the chest of silver that she had hidden for Claude, and she took consolation in the fact that one day he could be independent of his father. If he wanted to be free of his father's control, his grand-mother had provided a way. Angelique understood the wise old woman's reasoning very clearly now. She had been right.

"You will go back, Claude. I am sure of that." Angelique spoke with conviction. "We will help you, if we can."

"Perhaps we can return together," he said, looking up at Angelique.

Angelique sighed. "Maybe we can." But she had little hope of that now.

"Claude, you should go before your father misses you." As usual, Marie was the voice of logic, and Angelique nodded in agreement.

"Yes, maybe you can come back later." She reached over to put an arm around his little neck, and she pressed a kiss to his cold cheek. "We love you, Claude. Be brave today. Know that our hearts will be with you as you attend your mother's service. Remember, you will represent your grandmere."

He looked at her intently, and then slowly he began to nod. "You have given me hope. Thank you." He stood, still wringing his tam nervously between his hands. "I will be back."

She nodded, then watched him move quickly out of the tiny bedroom. When she heard the door into the hallway close, Angelique sank back on the pillow.

Marie lingered in the bedroom doorway. "He's such a wonderful little boy. How can he be the son of such a horrible man?"

"His mother must have been kind," Angelique said with a deep sigh. "She was just young and foolish, as you said. I'm sure she has regretted marrying Spencer Wolfe many times over the years. Or perhaps she saw another side of him, one that he keeps hidden from the rest of the world."

They were both quiet then, lost in thought. At last, Marie turned and walked into the living room. "I am going to get some tea for us. If we have to move out today, the landlady has been overpaid for one night's stay. We can at least have a good cup of tea."

Angelique tried to smile at her mother's wry humor, but she could not force her lips to make the effort.

Later in the day, Marie decided to ask the British soldier who guarded the house where the jail was and if they would be permitted to go there to see Philippe and Joseph.

The officer was curt with her, saying he was not at liberty to talk with her. However, the tenant in the second apartment overheard the conversation as he climbed the front steps, and later he slipped down the hall to knock on their door.

"I am so sorry for your plight," he said in a low voice, glancing back over his shoulder cautiously. "I am sympathetic to your cause." His voice dropped still lower so that Marie had to lean forward to understand him. "I will see what I can find out," he offered, looking worriedly at Marie.

"Please do not risk getting yourself in trouble," she whispered. "I fear we have brought enough problems with us. We do not want anyone else to be affected by our situation, even though I can assure you that our plight is terribly unfair."

"I am sure they have been taken to the main prison," the man said quickly.

"Then we may as well go there, too," Marie said with a sigh. "Can you tell us where it is?"

The man gave them directions. When he had left, Marie crossed her arms and stared at the floor, apparently deep in thought.

"Mother, what's going on?" Angelique called from the bed. Her empty teacup sat on the crate nightstand. The tea had been good, and she was grateful for its strength and warmth. For the first time since the soldiers came and arrested Joseph, she felt as though her blood was warm and flowing, instead of frozen ice.

Marie picked up her own cup and sipped her tea. "If we are traitors, perhaps they will put us in prison. Then we'll have free room and board," she said with a sarcasm that was untypical of her.

"That isn't funny, Mother. But, honestly, I wouldn't care if I were in prison or not. I feel our lives have ended."

"Stop feeling sorry for yourself," her mother scolded. "I must again remind you that there are people in worse condition than we. Your father and Joseph, for example. And poor Claude, losing the only parent to whom he was close."

Angelique nodded. With a sigh, she forced herself to get up from the bed. Her dress was rumpled and badly wrinkled, but she knew her mother was right. As always. She didn't know what they could do, but surely they would think of something. She wanted desperately to see Joseph again, and somehow her longing gave her hope. She wanted to see her father. They were all still alive, and at least they were together now in the same city.

"Do you have any idea what we can do?" she asked, looking at her mother.

"Not yet. I think all we can do is wait until the officers decide whether to toss us in prison or not."

Angelique moved stiffly into the living room. She looked from one end of the room to the other, and suddenly she felt as though she were going to smother. "Mother, I can't stay here. I have to get out. Walk. Think."

"The guard won't let you leave," her mother reminded her.

"He is at the front door, right? I am going out the back door and cut across the back lawns. Besides, what do I have to lose? I don't care if he shoots me." She bit her lip when she saw the hurt leap to her mother's face. "I'm sorry," she said, touching her mother's hand. "I didn't meant that. Not really. But I'd like to put on a cloak and go over to St. Mark's cemetery where Claude's mother will be buried this afternoon. My hair is still gray," she remembered, touching a thick strand. "Monsieur Wolfe won't recognize me."

"I don't know," her mother frowned.

"Well, I do," Angelique replied. "Excuse me, Mother, I don't mean to be disrespectful, but we must do as our own heart dictates. My heart tells me to go to Claude. Then maybe we will be able to see Father and Joseph."

Her mother sank onto the bed, taking Angelique's place. "I will not tell you what to do. Just be careful," she sighed. Stretching out on the bed, she crooked her arm over her forehead, hiding her face from view.

"I will be careful," Angelique said, as she pulled on

the heavy cloak. This time she reached down on the crate for her mother's worn gloves; she was tired of having her hands become half frozen. Slowly, she opened the door and peered out. The hall was empty, but she could see the Redcoat on the front porch. Surely another one would be stationed at the back door; she would soon find out.

She slipped into the kitchen, immensely relieved not to see the landlady lurking there. The woman looked like one who took afternoon naps, and with that hope, Angelique moved quickly to the back door and twisted the knob. Locked, but the key was in the door. As quietly as possible, she turned the key in the lock and waited as the big door slowly opened. She peered through the crack and saw a small porch, with steps leading to the back lawn. The lawn was heavily treed; she could easily slip through the trees, unless someone was watching.

Well, she would find out. Grabbing the market basket by the door, she eased the door shut, then hooked the straw basket on her arm and walked purposely across the lawn. A woman going to market. What was wrong with that? When she put her hand in her pocket, she found one shilling she had forgotten. The buns she had bought from Joseph were rapidly disappearing; perhaps she could find some apples and nuts, something that would keep them healthy and fill their stomachs.

Hurrying through the trees to the back street, she suddenly thought of the story of Robin Hood. She rushed through the trees, a definite mission in mind, and felt a strange kinship with the noble outlaw.

She stepped from the dense trees onto a cobblestone street, a narrow back lane that twisted and turned like a serpent. The shops here looked smaller, less affluent. As she passed a tailor's shop, her mind bolted back to Monsieur and Madame Harless, and she felt despair choking at her again. But she could not think of that hideous scene now. She had to obtain food and find the cemetery. The peel of the church bells told her it must be almost time for the burial.

She couldn't resist glancing into the tailor's shop, however. Inside, she saw a young boy standing beside an older man. The boy reminded her of Claude, though he was a little older. No doubt this boy was learning the trade, serving as an apprentice for seven years. Apprentices received clothes, lodging, and food, but few were ever paid in money. After their seven-year apprenticeship, they were considered master workmen. The young man she had spotted as she hurried by could someday have his own shop and teach another young apprentice the trade. *It's not a bad decided,* she mused, but she couldn't blame Claude for not wanting to pursue a trade for which he cared little.

But how can he learn to be a seaman instead? she wondered. Was his secret desire to become a sea captain so strong because he wanted to prove that he was more like his grandfather, Monsieur Russo, than his father, Spencer Wolfe?

Staring anxiously ahead, she saw only strange faces, and she was relieved that no one seemed to notice her in particular. Her thoughts lingered on Claude, who wanted only to return to Grand Pre, just as she did. *God, please let us go home,* she silently begged. Her prayer seemed impossible at this point, but she had to believe that God still heard and answered prayers. She and Joseph had come so close to their wedding, and then to be cruelly torn apart, when they finally had managed to find one another again. . .surely God would reward their love and patience in the end.

When she had run into Joseph's arms, she felt as though she had found the other half of herself. Now, she felt more like half a person, with a heart split down the middle, bleeding and sore. If she could not be with Joseph, could she ever be happy again? No, not happy, but she knew that she would somehow have to continue existing. She might feel that she only lived and breathed and knew whom she was when she was with Joseph, but others needed her as well. God expected her to be faithful to Him and to these other loved ones.

As she walked, she reminded herself of verses in her Bible: She was a child of God; she belonged to Him. No human was perfect; but God had blessed people with a special love, she knew that. If she never saw Joseph again, at least she had been wonderfully blessed.

She drew a deep breath of the crisp, salty air and told herself she could not lose heart. At least they had found one another, even though they were now separated by prison bars. *God, please tell us what to do; please work a miracle for us. Please!*

She approached a small church and quickly looked up to read the sign, but it was not Christ Church, where Claude had said his mother would be buried. An older gentleman was hobbling toward her, leaning heavily on his cane. When he glanced at her, she reached out and touched the sleeve of his coat.

"Could you please direct me to Christ Church?"

"Eh, what's that?" he asked, cupping a thin hand with prominent blue veins behind his right ear.

She glanced around, hoping she wasn't attracting attention. She moved closer to him, speaking directly into his ear. "Christ Church," she repeated slowly and carefully.

He nodded and jabbed a finger behind him. "Go down to the corner, take a right, and you'll walk straight to it." His wiry white brows arched as he looked her over. "It's a long walk, so mind your step. Just follow the bells. The bells in Christ Church are the best," he added, then leaned on his cane and hobbled on.

"Thank you," she called after him.

She picked up speed, her market basket swinging on her arm. She was enjoying the walk, she found, but then the dreary morning had turned to a sunny afternoon, casting its light on the dull gray hair that swung onto her shoulders. Good. Everyone would think she was an older woman; with a guilty start, she realized she had forgotten to walk like one.

She did not slow down, but rather lengthened her stride and leaned forward, like a healthy older woman. As soon as she turned the corner, she could hear the clear peel of the bells; looking far down to the end of the street, she spotted the lofty spire of the church. The bells seemed to draw her toward the church, where elegant carriages with their proper coachmen lined the cobblestone street. She slowed, aware the ceremony was already in progress.

As she neared the church, her eyes moved on to the adjoining cemetery. She could see a mound of fresh dirt in a choice corner of the cemetery. This must be where Claude's mother would be put to rest. She tried not to think of Madame Wolfe, for she could not afford to start weeping now; she could not call attention to herself in any way. Claude, above all, was her concern now. If she could just let him know she was near, perhaps that would give him some measure of comfort.

Just before she reached the church, the doors opened and well-dressed people began to emerge. She stepped under the awning of a shop and drew back from their view. Still, she could watch. She saw the flowers and the casket, and the grim Monsieur Wolfe with Claude at his side. Another woman, who vaguely resembled Spencer Wolfe, was carrying the little girl, who was sobbing pitifully. Angelique's heart twisted at the sight of the crying child and the frail figure of Claude with his downcast head.

Why did his mother have to die? It seemed so unfair. There was no understanding life or its strange mysteries. One simply had to go on doing one's best to survive.

More solemn people followed Claude and his family, their heads bowed in grief or respect, all looking very dignified and proper as the procession continued around the side of the church to the cemetery. Angelique stepped out from under the awning and crept toward the crowd. Her cloak certainly was not the fine quality of those the other women wore, but then she spotted the maid and the cook, toward the back of the line. Their cloaks were not any better than her mother's, just newer;

hopefully, she could blend in with the servants. They were not looking in her direction, because they seemed to be transfixed by the sight of their employer and his sad children beside the fine mahogany casket with its mounds of flowers.

She quickened her pace to join in the last stragglers of the procession, careful to keep her head down. Suddenly aware of the market basket on her arm, she paused and placed it beside the chimney of the church. She didn't think anyone would steal a simple market basket, but what difference did it make? She might never make it to the market, particularly if Spencer Wolfe recognized her.

That did not seem likely, however, because he seemed to be in a daze, moving in a slow stilted fashion, as though his body were a machine that had no sense of what was going on. Clearly, Angelique realized, he was heartbroken.

The procession was nearing the grave site, and the family was ushered onto a cushioned wooden bench directly in front of it. The other benches, she noticed, held no cushions. Slipping unobtrusively onto the back row, she quickly took her seat on the last wooden bench, a comfortable distance from the Wolfe family—and yet she longed to let Claude know she was here. Perhaps she would find a way later.

Pressing her cloak against her legs so that an older couple could move past her to the center of the bench, she spotted a pair of spectacles lying in the grass. Leaning down, she picked up the spectacles and looked around her. No one appeared to be looking for a lost object, and as she examined the spectacles again, she saw the dirt encrusted on the edges of the frames. Apparently, the spectacles had been here for some time. She could use them perfectly to her advantage. Reaching into her pocket, she withdrew the lace handkerchief. Her gloved hands gently brushed the dirt from the frames, and then she used a clean corner of the handkerchief to rub the lenses clean. Slipping them under her cloak, she ran the surface of the lenses back and forth across her soft wrinkled skirt.

The minister had begun to speak, and all heads were reverently turned toward him. In a slow and careful gesture, she lifted the spectacles and hooked the curve of the frames around her ears. Everything suddenly became slightly blurred, as though she were looking through a crystal glass of shimmering water. Still, she could see the people around her easily enough.

Slowly she shook the hood back from her head, and with what she hoped appeared to be an idle gesture, she smoothed down her long gray hair. If only she had given any thought to this, she would have secured her hair in a proper bun. But with her hair covering her face and the spectacles on her nose, hopefully Spencer Wolfe, in his daze of grief, would never recognize her. And perhaps not even the maid or cook would realize who she was. But she knew Claude's shrewd eye would find her. He knew her features too well; and he knew that her hair was dyed gray.

She sat up straighter, aware that the couple next to her was whispering loudly. "Poor Spencer. She was such a pretty young woman."

And a sweet woman, Angelique could have added.

She knew that had to be true from the character of Claude and his grandmother. She tried to see over the shoulders of those in front of her, to the front row, but little Claude was too short for her to observe. She did, however, see the rigid set of Wolfe's shoulders in his tailored dark suit and proper hat. Above the minister's deep calm voice, she could hear the loud sobs of the little girl, and she felt a stab of pain.

Suddenly, she wanted more than anything to take care of those children, at least until she could be with Joseph. She belonged with Claude—but could she manage it somehow?

Heads were bent now, as the minister offered a prayer, and soon the casket was lowered and the family was led away from the scene. Apparently, Wolfe had declined the option of staying to watch his wife's casket covered over with earth. The little girl was practically hysterical, and Angelique could understand why the family would choose to leave this scene as soon as possible.

As the family passed her seat, she stared long and hard at Claude, hoping somehow to capture the sad eyes in the downcast face. He did not look her way, however. The crowd was standing. On an impulse, not stopping to think, Angelique caught up with Claude and gently touched his shoulder.

His little head jerked up in surprise, and for a moment, his expression did not change. Then his eyes widened in recognition. He stopped walking and looked from her to the cook and maid as they passed, merely nodding in her direction. They had not recognized her either! She decided to press her luck and walk beside Claude, whose taut face suddenly relaxed as he slyly slid his hand in hers. She squeezed his fingers.

"You were such a good student," she said, loud enough to be heard, careful to pronounce her words exactly as she had heard the people of Boston speaking. She had always had a sharp ear for language, and she knew she could pass for a local if she kept her voice low and soft.

Claude's head jerked back to her and his eyes widened again. "Mrs. Witherspoon, I want you to meet my little sister. And maybe Father."

Angelique's breath caught in her throat. If Claude were willing to take this risk, however, she would follow his lead.

They had reached the carriage now, and the little girl's sobbing had softened to a whimper. Suddenly, Spencer Wolfe turned and looked back at Claude.

"Father, Mrs. Witherspoon was an assistant at St. Mark's last year. She was a great help to me in penmanship."

Wolfe looked from Claude to Angelique, who tilted her head back and squinted at him through the blurred vision of the spectacles. She extended her hand. "How do you do? I am so sorry for your loss," she said, speaking in a voice that sounded appropriately proper to her ears. "Claude was my favorite student."

Wolfe lingered a moment, staring at Claude. Clearly, Wolfe was surprised that for the first time since his mother's death Claude had responded to someone; this seemed to please even the hardened Wolfe.

"I wish Mrs. Witherspoon could come for a visit and help me with my alphabet," Claude said. "I have not been doing so well. And she could read nursery rhymes to Elizabeth, as Mother used to do."

Wolfe's expression changed again, and Angelique saw the raw pain in his face.

"I have read my little students many stories." She thought of the stories she had made up for the children in Grand Pre. "It was a great pleasure to see their little faces when they listened." She added carefully, "I wish to do anything I can to help Claude and his little sister."

Wolfe nodded. "It would be appreciated. Do come."

Then he turned on his heel and headed toward the carriage. Claude asked loudly, "Would you come tomorrow? We can spend some time with my penmanship and then you can read a nursery rhyme to Elizabeth."

The maid glanced Angelique's way again, but she still showed no recognition. Angelique could barely believe her luck. She wanted so much to be with Claude and his sister. She had a feeling that if she could get inside the house, she could somehow work to the advantage of Joseph and her father.

"I will see you tomorrow," she said to Claude.

"Ten o'clock in the morning is a good time for Elizabeth," Wolfe said brusquely over his shoulder.

"Yes, sir. I will come at that hour," she replied, her head lowered slightly in respect. Then she turned and forced herself to walk slowly through the crowd.

sixteen

"Angelique, you cannot go there. This is insane!" Her mother gripped her shoulders as they stood in the center of the shabby living room, surrounded by box-crate furniture; the remaining buns were their only sustenance, but both of them were too agitated to eat.

"Mother, this is the only way, don't you see? If I can be a friend to Claude and his sister, I may have a chance to help Father and Joseph."

"I don't want anything to happen to you," her mother said, her voice breaking, her eyes filling with tears. All the strength she had demonstrated over the past weeks evaporated at the prospect of losing her daughter.

"I promise you, I will be safe. Claude will not allow his father to harm me, and I will win his sister's affection, as well."

Neither slept that night, although they huddled close beneath the thin blanket, each breath a tiny cloud drifting into the cold darkness. When finally the darkness softened and Angelique could make out a thin shaft of light gray beyond the ugly drapes, she slipped gently from the bed. Her mother's breathing was slow and even, and when Angelique cast a glance at her, she saw that her mother's features had finally relaxed; for now she was at peace.

Angelique dressed quickly, remembering the one last

shilling in her pocket. She would buy tea today, for she knew how her mother enjoyed her tea. If they had only tea and bread, that would be ample, for now hope blazed like a warm fire inside her frozen body. Surely, something good would happen today.

She brushed her hair back and wound it into a bun, securing it with her mother's hairpins. Then she ran a dry handkerchief over her face and reached into her mother's tiny poke of herbs for two peppermint leaves. She ran one up and down her dress, pleased by the fragrance. The other leaf she popped in her mouth, swishing it over her teeth and under her tongue, hoping to freshen her breath.

Poking in the tiny closet, she spotted a little hat in the far corner of the upper shelf, left behind, no doubt, by the cook. She brushed it off and put it on her head. She longed to bathe in warm water, but that was like wishing to be home again, so she pushed aside the wish for now and reached for her mother's cloak. After a moment's hesitation, she grabbed the cloak beside it as well, her own, and tiptoed to her mother's bedside. Carefully and gently, she spread the extra cover over her mother's body, hoping to warm her.

Then Angelique slipped quietly out the door, taking slow measured steps on the tips of her feet until she reached the back door. The cold key rattled loudly in its lock; for a moment she froze, various excuses flying through her mind if the officer or anyone else rushed into the hall to investigate.

To her immense relief, the house remained still and quiet. With the patience of Job, she opened the door inch by inch until there was enough space to slip through; ever so gently, she closed it behind her. Once again, she forced herself to be slow and deliberate, although her urge was to flee quickly into the dim gray dawn.

She silently thanked the cook for the proper little hat, and as her fingers closed over the spectacles in her pocket, she thanked God and some poor soul for leaving them in her path yesterday. For the sake of her vision, however, she would not put them on until she reached the Wolfe residence.

She was shivering by the time she reached the Wolfes' street, more from nervousness than cold. Her eyes nervously scanned the front of the houses, expecting to see servants going about their business, but then she realized that the hour was still too early. She saw through a window that several people had gathered in a small tea shop on the corner, and she thought she recognized some of the Wolfe servants. Placing her spectacles on, she reached into her other pocket and withdrew her last shilling.

Please God, let this be enough, she silently prayed. To her relief, the shilling not only bought her a large cup of tea, but a packet of tea leaves to take home to her mother. And if she could find spectacles and tea and a way to get to Claude, surely she could round up a kettle of water to place on their tiny hearth with its pitiful little fire.

seventeen

"I am so glad to be near you again," Claude whispered. They huddled close together over a tablet and plumed pen on a small desk in Mr. Wolfe's study.

"And I with you," Angelique whispered, glancing over her shoulder to reassure herself the door was still closed. "When can I meet your sister?"

Claude's little face turned upward, and she saw again the familiar expression of sadness in his eyes. "I hope you can help Elizabeth. I have asked her if you could read to her, but she didn't seem interested."

Angelique thought for a moment, remembering the children gathered around her at the village square. "Do you happen to know her favorite nursery rhyme?"

A frown knitted Claude's little forehead as he considered the question. "She has a picture book she likes to look at."

"Perfect," Angelique said with relief. She could spin a story from the pictures. "Tell her to choose her favorite and I will read that one to her. Go see if she would like to see me now."

Soon Claude was back, his face more cheerful now. Angelique followed him into the hall and up the long, winding staircase. Careful to grip the rail, like one fearful of falling, whose vision was not as good in old age, she took slow, careful steps, in case anyone watched from a doorway below.

Claude led her halfway down a large hall whose floorboards were warmed by a rich Oriental rug, the walls decorated with richly colored oil paintings. Halfway down the corridor, his steps slowed, and he turned the knob of the room Angelique remembered from her brief stay in the house.

Elizabeth waited inside, looking small and frightened in the deep four-poster bed. The little girl said nothing, but Angelique sensed that she was measuring her with her eyes. Angelique recognized Spencer Wolfe's caution in the little face, and the girl's features closely resembled her father's, making her less attractive than Claude, who looked nothing like his father. Claude must have been his mother's son, Angelique decided, for his name was French while Elizabeth was decidedly British.

"Here is the book," Claude said, thrusting a leather-bound volume into her hands.

"Thank you," she said, studying the delicate artwork on the cover of the book. Then, looking back at the little girl who had not yet smiled, she moved toward her and settled slowly into the armchair beside the bed. She sensed that she must proceed slowly and carefully with the little girl, who seemed far less friendly than Claude. Perhaps a story would win her trust, and so Angelique opened the book.

Angelique's reading was limited, but her imagination was good. She studied the book's illustrations for a moment, and then, settling back in the chair and adjusting her frames, she began to speak, slowly and gently, weaving a tender story she hoped would touch the little girl's heart.

She had been telling stories for over an hour when suddenly she was conscious of another presence in the room. The little girl bolted up in bed, her arms outstretched. "Father!" she said, her features holding a joy that Claude had not demonstrated in the presence of his father.

"Elizabeth, you look as though you are enjoying yourself!" The sound of Spencer Wolfe's voice sent a chill down Angelique's spine, and she automatically stiffened, lifting a hand to adjust her glasses. She had a headache from peering over the top of the blurred glasses, but the headache would be nothing compared to the torture this man could administer if he discovered her identity.

"She has been telling me the nicest stories," Elizabeth said, a tiny smile creeping over her pale lips. This pleased Angelique, and the stiff Spencer Wolfe suddenly stepped closer to the bed, his face revealing pleasure for the first time since Angelique had met him.

"I will give you privacy now with your daughter, sir," she said, coming to her feet, careful to grip the arm of the chair and move slowly.

Avoiding his face, she had almost reached the door when Elizabeth called out to her. "When are you coming back to read to me?"

Angelique hesitated, her hand on the knob.

"We do not want to impose on Miss. . . ," Wolfe faltered, obviously having forgotten the name Claude had mentioned at the funeral.

"Mrs. Witherspoon," Angelique quickly supplied.

"And it is no imposition, sir," she said, only half turning her head. "I have. . .lost my husband and I appreciate the opportunity to fill my lonely days." She spoke in a deeper voice, imitating a British accent as closely as possible. She hoped he believed her.

"Then please come again," he invited. "Claude said you worked with him for an hour on his penmanship. He seems pleased. I will be happy to pay you."

"It isn't necessary," she answered humbly.

"I insist. My children are. . .of utmost importance to me."

Angelique turned her face a fraction more, allowing him only a glimpse of her profile, framed by gray hair and thick glasses. "Then I shall return tomorrow at ten, if you wish."

There was a pause, and from the corner of her eye, she could see the little girl nodding approval before Wolfe spoke again. "Please do. I'll have Cook prepare lunch next time."

❧

Cook did prepare a lunch for her the next day, and Wolfe left an envelope for her with three shillings inside. Angelique sent a silent prayer of thanks winging upward, for she and her mother had nothing now. Carefully, she placed the shillings in her pocket and smiled down into Claude's face.

"We will work on your alphabet again," she said. "You are doing much better."

Angelique continued to go daily to the Wolfe house, staying longer each day, slowly winning the heart of Elizabeth, who now laughed at the funny stories Angelique told, stories her mother and grandmother had told her when she was a child herself. Angelique had nearly exhausted her own imagination, however; she could think of no new stories about princesses and elves and golden carriages. So, on her next trip, she took her Bible with her, determined to begin with a children's version of Noah and the ark. Her mother had taught her well, and she knew many Bible stories by heart.

On the last day of the second week, as she approached the door, Claude jerked it open as though he had been waiting a long time. She stopped, clutching the handrail, fearing the worst. But his eyes were shining and a huge smile was on his little face.

"Elizabeth told Father last night that it was the cook we used to have who brought the sickness. She said Mother found out the woman was sick and ordered her to leave at once. She gave her money to care for herself, but she wanted the woman out of the house before her illness spread." Claude's small face sobered. "It must have been too late. Father confronted the kitchen staff and they admitted the cook had already prepared several meals before Mother noticed the cook was feverish. Yesterday, her husband came to the back door to say she had died. His face was marked with scars, as well."

Claude's eyes danced now, and his hand squeezed hers. "Now Father knows it was not the 'older man,' as everyone calls him—they are speaking of Monsieur Boudreau—who brought the sickness to our house. He regrets having Joseph and Monsieur Boudreau arrested."

"Would he change his mind and help them?" Angelique asked, her heart racing, her emotions leaping with hope. She realized how harsh the man was, and she hurtled back to despair. Spencer Wolfe was not one to admit a mistake.

"I asked him that," Claude said, his smile disappearing. "He does not wish to anger the officers or bring suspicion upon himself."

Angelique's heart sank.

"But he is thinking it over, I can tell," Claude offered hopefully. "Perhaps we can find a way. . . ."

Just the perhaps was enough to brighten her day, and Angelique gazed longingly into space. "If only he would free them. . . ."

"If only we could all return to Grand Pre," he said, his shoulders slumping again.

Something in his tone made Angelique turn to stare at him. "Have you told him you wish to go?" she asked incredulously.

He nodded. "Last night after Elizabeth told him about Cook, I could not refrain from crying. Father demanded to know what was wrong. I told him your parents and Joseph were the kindest people I had ever known and that Grandmere wanted me to return to her. And that more than anything, I wanted to live there and be a seaman."

He paused and his little body heaved with a deep sigh. "Father does not like the idea. He wants me to follow in his trade and be a silversmith. I hate it," Claude blurted, the anger and bitterness contorting his features. "And soon I will grow to hate him, as well."

"No, Claude," Angelique murmured, smoothing her hand over his head, "do not hate. Please. You must not let hate into your heart." But she couldn't blame the child for being hurt and angry. Couldn't his father see what he was doing to his son?

As she climbed the steps to the upper floor with Claude at her side, Angelique thought of everything he had just said to her. "I am too upset to work on my alphabet today," he told her, and Angelique nodded.

"So am I."

"We have one hope," he said, clutching her sleeve.

They stopped halfway up the stairs as Angelique turned to him and asked, "What is it?"

"Elizabeth likes you very much. Father worships her, just as he did my mother. I am not like them," he said, his sigh heavy again.

As she saw the pain in his eyes, Angelique wondered how Spencer Wolfe could reject this wonderful little boy. Why had God allowed such tragedy to rob him of his childhood? He had obviously been unhappy ever since they left Grand Pre.

"Perhaps if Elizabeth asked to go visit Grandmere this spring," Claude said after they had quietly climbed the stairs, "then Father would allow me to go, too. I will tell her how wonderful it is there. And you could accompany us as a chaperone, you and your mother."

Angelique's hopes leapt, and then reality hit. "But we cannot leave Boston with our men in prison. And the officers have seized our lands by now. We have nowhere to go in Grand Pre."

"To Grandmere's house!" Claude exclaimed. "She has plenty of land, and she would gladly share with you. Your father and Joseph could build a cabin."

"But how can they be free? How can we ever return?"

Angelique wished desperately that Claude's desire could be granted. If only somehow they could be reunited and go to their beloved homeland. But it seemed impossible.

Then she remembered something her mother had told her as a child, when her little kitten was very sick and Angelique feared the kitten would not get well. "We will pray for your kitten," her mother had said. "Nothing is impossible with God." Sure enough, with enough warm milk and loving care, the kitten had slowly regained its health. Angelique smiled at the memory. God had loved her enough to listen to a child's prayer for a sick kitten—surely He would hear her prayers now.

Deep in thought, she clutched the rail and continued to climb the stairs. She was coming to the Wolfe house daily, being paid for something she loved doing, and she had miraculously won the heart of Elizabeth. She had even impressed Spencer Wolfe. Surely, these things must show that God's hand was at work. *But Spencer Wolfe is only impressed with me because he thinks I am Mrs. Witherspoon,* the voice of reason spoke in her head.

And then, suddenly, she knew what she had to do. She had to face Spencer Wolfe and tell him who she really was. With God to give her courage, she would dare to be honest. She would tell Wolfe everything about Claude's inheritance and how she had buried the silver for his grandmother. She would be honest and forthright, which she instinctively knew was the only thing Spencer Wolfe would truly respect.

eighteen

"Do you, Angelique Boudreau, take this man, Joseph Landry, to be your lawful wedded husband?"

Angelique was staring up at him, her brown eyes filled with love, her voice soft and gentle as she spoke.

"I do," she said with conviction.

Their life together seemed to flash before Joseph's eyes, a wondrous blessed miracle. Angelique stood by his side, dressed in a beautiful white dress that accented her delicate features and lush dark hair, her eyes full of kindness. He was the luckiest man alive. He swallowed, trying to keep his emotions in check, as he turned back to the minister, ready to answer his part of the wedding vows.

But suddenly the minister faded away, as though a gray mist had swirled over him, taking him into thin air. Where had he gone? What had happened? Puzzled, he turned to Angelique. But the same gray cloud had taken her away, as well; and now all he could see was the lace edge of a ruffle at the bottom of her dress.

"Angelique!" He reached out for her, to save her from whatever strange fog had enveloped the coast. Had the sea overflowed the dikes? "Angelique!" he shouted again, trying to grope his way through the fog.

"Joseph!" It was a man's voice, not the voice of the minister, and he felt a pressure on his shoulder.

His subconscious told him to hold on, to stay where he was, that he must remain in that chapel with Angelique, clear the fog, continue his vows so they could marry and live as man and wife.

"Joseph, you are dreaming," the voice spoke again. A gentle voice that held love and sorrow all mingled together in the same soft plea.

Before he opened his eyes, the nightmare of reality hit him, and for a moment, he wanted to die. Philippe was there beside him, he knew that. They were in the depths of a dank Boston prison, and their chance of ever seeing daylight again did not look good.

He took a long, deep breath and nodded, but still he did not open his eyes. He couldn't force himself to do that, for then he would have to face the grimness of his hideous world.

Philippe was whispering in his ear, trying to encourage him without the other prisoners hearing the words. "At least they have found us. They know we are here. They will find a way to get us out. And we have the knowledge that they are well, they have survived."

The words crept into Joseph's tormented brain as he tried to find hope in what Philippe said. Philippe had been just as upset as Joseph had been about being arrested. And Philippe had not even had the chance to glimpse his beloved wife, let alone hold her in his arms.

But although Joseph was grateful that at least he had seen Angelique and spoken with her, he was also tortured by the memory of actually holding her in his arms. He had found her softer, lovelier, more appealing than ever. Never in his life had Joseph wanted anything so much as to be with Angelique, however he could.

When the officers had found him underneath the bed and ordered him out, he had been tempted to fight back. He was naturally strong and well-muscled, and even without a gun, he had hopes of overtaking the two men physically. But a quick glance at Marie and Angelique had kept him from doing anything rash. If he did not go peacefully, the officers might shoot all of them. He would rather die in a prison or hang at the gallows than have either woman harmed.

But if missing Angelique had been painful before he saw her, it was a nightmare now. Every bone in his body ached to be with her, and he felt as though he had a deep bleeding pain in his heart; he knew now what the word heartbreak meant. He would not wish this torment on any other human being. He hated no one that much. . . except Spencer Wolfe. His lips twisted as he thought of the man who had betrayed them.

"Quiet down," a voice thundered. "You, old man. Get back in your cot."

At that Joseph came awake, his protective instincts overcoming his pain for the moment. His eyes flew open, his fists balled, his blood pounded through his body. Philippe stared down at Joseph, his face bleak in the dim cell where the distant glow of a lantern from down the narrow hall cast an eerie light. With a sigh, Philippe got to his feet.

Joseph broke into a cold sweat as Philippe returned to his cot. How much more of this could they endure? Hour after hour, as the long night crept by, he lay staring at the ceiling. He could not even find the strength to pray.

nineteen

Claude made the appointment for her. She told him to make sure that his father understood this was urgent, that it concerned a matter of grave importance. Of course, Mr. Wolfe would think that his ten o'clock meeting was with Mrs. Witherspoon, the woman who had so lovingly cared for his children the past month. Without a doubt, he would assume that she wanted to discuss some aspect of his children's care with him.

The bitter February cold tore at her cloak and turned her cheeks raw as she hurried to the Wolfe home. Claude opened the door, looking anxious, but she merely smiled at him and gently touched his cheek with her gloved hand. He flinched slightly from the cold and hurried her inside.

Spencer Wolfe was seated at his desk, looking small and rather vulnerable, she thought as she entered the room. He quickly stood to his feet. "Please sit down, Mrs. Witherspoon." He indicated the armchair.

A fire blazed in the fireplace, and she glanced gratefully toward it. She was frozen to the bone, but at least she could enjoy periods of warmth during the day, while her mother had to hover over the tiny fireplace, wrapped in a blanket, shivering and sipping hot tea. That memory strengthened her resolve as she quietly removed her cloak, hooked it on the coat tree, and went to the chair.

She was not wearing the spectacles today; although her hair was still gray, the pretense was over.

He stared at her curiously, as though really seeing her for the first time. For a moment, a puzzled expression crossed his face, and then she watched his eyes move to her gray hair, as though seeking assurance that she was not whom he suspected.

"The gray will wash out," she said evenly, dropping the British accent. "I have something very important to tell you that concerns Claude." She came right to the point before he could throw her out. "But first you have to hear me out. I am Angelique Boudreau, as you are beginning to suspect, I am sure. My mother and I have always been kind to Claude and—"

"And you've been kind to my daughter," he interrupted, staring at her as though nothing made sense. "You could have come here and harmed the children out of retaliation for. . ." He faltered, then fell silent, his eyes never leaving her face.

"For what you did to Joseph and my father? I could have sought revenge for your actions, but I would not. You see, Monsieur Wolfe, I will not let myself be a slave to hatred. Nor do I believe in murder or theft, both of which the British officers have committed against your wife's people. They have suffered horribly, even though they built the dikes and cleared the land that you now find so valuable."

"I did not agree with. . ." He broke off, correcting himself. "I had nothing to do with the deportation."

"But you had everything to do with having Joseph and my father thrown in prison, and I can only pray to God that they are still alive."

At those words, he dropped his head.

"I truly love Claude and your daughter Elizabeth," Angelique continued. "My mother loved your wife, although I was too young to know her well. But I did know Madame Russo, and we have been neighbors and friends for all of my life."

He cleared his throat. "My wife spoke well of your family," he acknowledged, his voice low and unsteady.

"And I made a promise to Madame Russo I intend to keep."

He looked up suddenly, wondering what was coming next.

"She knew Claude wanted to return to Grand Pre and she has left an inheritance for him. If her land has been taken—"

"I—er—don't think—"

"Even so, Claude still has something valuable," she continued smoothly. "Madame Russo asked me to tell no one, but I believe you are a man who respects honesty, and I feel it is my only chance to make things right for. . .all of us."

"Go on." He leaned forward, his hands clasped tightly on the desk.

"Before we left Grand Pre, while you were finding a nurse, Madame Russo gave me a valuable chest of silver to hide for Claude. When he returns to Grand Pre, it will be his to use for land or whatever he wishes. Of course, he wishes to live there, but that may not be your ambition for him. In any case, I did as she asked. I buried the chest of silver on my baby brother's grave. It will be safe there until Claude claims it again. I plan to tell Claude this."

Spencer Wolfe stared at her, his jaw dropping. "Are you telling me that you hid a chest of silver for Claude? And you and your mother have been starving to death?"

She didn't know how he knew that, but it was true. She nodded, not mentioning the torture of the cold or the dark fear that followed them like a shadow.

"Why would you do this?" he asked, his voice so low she could hardly hear him.

"Because I am a woman of honor, just as your wife was. I love Claude as though he were the brother he helped me bury. I want what is best for him, and he believes he will never be happy here, only in Grand Pre."

"But he's only a child. . . ." The gruffness returned to his voice.

"Can a child care for a sick blind woman, build fires, cook meals, protect three women, as he did his grandmother and us? Can a child go among the soldiers seeking help, without fearing for his own life? And can a child bear the type of burden he has carried for so long, the one that has grown heavier with the loss of his mother?"

He looked up at her. "What burden is that?"

"The burden of knowing that his own father apparently does not love him."

Spencer Wolfe passed a hand over his face and sat for a moment with his eyes closed. The room was silent, except for the crackle of the fire. Angelique watched him for a moment, and then she continued.

"I have been honest with you and now I am pleading

for the life of my father and my fiancé. We are willing to stay in Boston and work hard, if only you will free our men from prison and allow Joseph and me to marry."

He opened his eyes and looked at her thoughtfully. "When I first saw you, I was reminded of my wife that day in the shop when I first met her. She was young and smart with a dash about her that made her appear stronger than other women. And you are strong like she was, and very brave. I am astonished that you would come to me and tell me this. You could have gone back someday and reclaimed the silver and bought back your land and—"

She put up her hand. "I told you, I do not believe in stealing and that is precisely what I would be doing if I were to take Claude's silver. I was taught to treat others as I would want to be treated myself; I have tried very hard to do that. It has been difficult not to despise the Redcoats—but I know it is not the men but rather the war raging about us that has brought evil to everyone."

She paused and drew a deep breath to deliver her final request, the one which meant life or death to her. "You have the power to go to the prison and buy our men's freedom. We will work hard for you. Joseph is an artisan with wood, and my father—"

"I am aware of their talents. And you are proposing to work for me as well? You and your mother?"

She hesitated. "If you wish."

"Tell me something." His eyes flicked over each feature of her face. "Does freeing your father and fiancé mean enough to you that you would agree to be my wife?"

She gasped, totally shocked by his words. She had not expected this, and for a moment she was tempted to agree, but she knew she could never love any man but Joseph. Slowly, she shook her head.

"You do not want that, Mr. Wolfe. I would be robbing you of what you deserve. You need a wife who loves you. I. . .love Joseph."

He leaned back in the chair, saying nothing more. "And if I refuse to do what you have asked?"

She lifted her face, looking him squarely in the eye. "I do not believe Madame Russo's daughter would chose to marry a man that cruel. And I believe that as dear as Claude and Elizabeth are, they must have something of their father in them. At heart, you must be a good and decent man. I do not believe you will stoop to bribery or use my words as weapons against me." Her voice had grown weak, but she forced herself to finish her speech with conviction.

Realizing she had depleted all the strength from her body, she rose shakily and walked across to retrieve her cloak. "I'm sure you'll want to think about this," she said with a sigh. "Claude knows where we live. I would still like to see Claude and Elizabeth again, regardless of your decision."

She put on her cloak and shook the thick gray hair back from her face, relieved that now she could wash out the gray. She walked toward the door, her teeth sinking into her bottom lip, every nerve strained to hear him speak a word, to say something to give her hope. But he said nothing. She opened the door and walked out into the hall where Claude was nervously pacing.

She knelt beside him, hugging him hard. "I have told your father the truth. You know where we live if he changes his mind. Please pray for Joseph and Father," she added, fighting the lump in her throat.

Then she forced herself to stand and walk out the door. As she descended the steps and faced the frigid cold, she saw from the corner of her eye that a curtain had parted, and she knew Spencer Wolfe was watching her walk away.

twenty

Joseph looked and responded like one whose mind was gone. He had spoken little as he did what he was told, his manner stilted and unemotional. Unlike the old Joseph Landry, he now seemed more like a man who had lost all life and hope. Philippe, desperately thin, pale, and obviously unwell, was the one who now assumed the responsibility for keeping them alive.

Neither Philippe nor Joseph knew what day it was, only that it was winter. One long freezing gray day slowly disappeared into another, and none of the prisoners bothered keeping up with the day of the week, or the month, or even the year. They plodded through their backbreaking labor and endured.

Now and then a new prisoner brought news from the outside world. The French and Indians were losing the war to the British, now that the fighting had moved closer to Boston, and they all knew that the French prisoners would be held captive as long as there was a conflict. From the sketchy reports that Joseph could overhear, he thought there would always be a conflict, even though none of the Acadians wanted war or any part of it. They simply wanted to return to their beloved homeland.

One midmorning a guard came to Joseph, then to Philippe, and asked them to report to Sergeant Hastings.

Puzzled but afraid to ask questions, the two men laid down their tools and followed the guard. They were led down a long corridor, and then another, one they had never seen before, and finally they ended up in the warden's office.

The stately warden sat behind his desk, and an even more dignified gentleman sat opposite him. Philippe gasped out loud at the sight of the second man, and Joseph turned curiously to him. Philippe obviously recognized Sergeant Hastings's visitor.

The warden cleared his throat. "This man is Spencer Wolfe," he said, and now Joseph also gasped. He had never met Mr. Wolfe before, as Philippe had always been the one to contact him. "He is a prominent silversmith here," the warden continued, "and he has just purchased your freedom. You are now under his care as his servants. You will go with him and do as you are told."

Joseph stared at the middle-aged little man who was dressed in fine tailored clothing, every strand of his white wig properly in place. Mr. Wolfe leaned across the desk and deposited a cloth bag filled with money. Then he stood.

"Shall we go?"

Joseph could not believe this was actually happening, but a small smile hovered on Philippe's face as he looked at Spencer Wolfe.

No one spoke as Joseph and Philippe followed the dignified gentleman down the muddy boardwalk that seemed to go on forever, until at last they reached the door to freedom. A guard unlocked the gate. It swung open, and for the first time in weeks, Joseph felt a ray of hope return to his broken heart. He lifted his eyes to the blue sky and silently thanked God. He had not abandoned them after all. Even when Joseph had allowed himself to be drowned by despair and hatred, God had not forgotten them.

❧

Marie and Angelique sat in the parlor, too nervous to think or feel or even hope. Claude had come for them early this morning, saying only that his father wished to see them. Apparently, he had news of Philippe and Joseph, and he instructed them to return with Claude to the Wolfe home. They were to be in his parlor promptly at ten bells.

They sat stiffly on the settee, hands clasped, their thoughts racing with a million unanswered questions. Still, they dared not venture conversation. Claude had been relegated to his sister's room, and now they were alone in the huge room that was filled with fine mahogany furnishings. A crystal chandelier hung over their heads, and a valuable Persian rug was at their feet. A cheerful fire blazed in the fireplace, but Angelique could not keep herself from shivering.

Although their once-good dark dresses were now no more than rags, at least they were clean and unwrinkled. *Hopefully,* Angelique thought, *the mint sachet will compensate for our lack of bathing facilities.* Quick splashes of freezing water from a small pan were the nearest they had come to a bath since they had left Grand Pre.

They heard the sound of carriage wheels rolling over the cobblestone drive, and Angelique jumped to her feet. Marie's hand shot out, however, gripping a fold of her daughter's skirt, keeping her from flying to the door.

"Monsieur Wolfe said to wait right here," her mother said in her usual steady voice. "We will do exactly that."

Angelique was torn between the hope that Mr. Wolfe might have responded to her plea for help and the bitter reminder that he had mentioned marriage. Would he again ask her to consider his offer? She had decided, in the wee hours of the night, after many tears, that if she needed to marry Spencer Wolfe to free her parents and Joseph, then she would do so. And she would force herself to be an obedient wife—but never, ever would she feel any passion for a man other than Joseph.

She had pelted Claude with questions on the ride over in the carriage, but he seemed to know nothing. "Father has spent the past two days out of the house on business," the boy had replied. "It was only this morning that I saw him for the first time. He asked me then to direct the driver to your place and bring you back. He has told me nothing." Claude's face was bleak. "I have no idea what he is plotting."

❧

When Joseph and Philippe followed Spencer Wolfe into the parlor, they stood still, momentarily stunned by the warmth and bright colors. Then Joseph saw Angelique, and his eyes devoured her face. She leapt to her feet, her gaze hungrily seeking each feature of his face. Joseph wanted to jump forward and grab her in his arms, but he forced himself to stand still, waiting for Wolfe to speak.

Spencer Wolfe looked uncomfortable for a moment, and then he crossed the room and picked up an envelope that lay on a small marble table. Joseph saw his gaze move from person to person, and then he cleared his throat.

"I have here," he said, opening the envelope, "the purchase of the deed of your land, Mr. Landry."

Joseph heard Angelique gasp, but her mother motioned for her to be quiet. Their eyes were all fixed on Spencer Wolfe as he continued.

"You are free to return to your homeland. All of you. The document is properly notarized. My only condition is that you also care for the adjoining land that will one day be my son's." He sighed, and his gaze dropped. "I know that Claude will want to return to Grand Pre with you, but I feel he is still too young. He and I. . .we need to get to know each other better. However, in a few years, when he is older, he may do as he wishes. In the meantime, I would be grateful if you will care for his grandmother. Assure her that Claude will return."

"That will keep her alive," Marie said softly. "Of course we will care for her."

Wolfe's eyes moved from Marie to her husband. "Thank you. I believe you are people of honor. I–I must apologize for my part in your hardship. To make amends, allow me to provide you with an adequate wardrobe before you depart for your home."

❧

No one knew quite what to say; they were all too stunned, Angelique realized. In the end, Claude was the one who broke the reverent silence. Apparently, he had been listening at the door, for now the door burst open and he rushed across the room, throwing his arms around his father's waist. "Thank you, Father. This is a kind and wonderful thing you have done, and I shall always respect you for it. Grandmere will be so pleased." He paused, his eyes lifted to his father's face, and then he added shyly, "I know Mother is smiling down from heaven."

Tears rose in Spencer Wolfe's eyes as his arms slowly encircled Claude's narrow shoulders. "Thank you, Son. Just seeing your happiness confirms my decision that this was the right thing to do."

"It was, Papa; it was," he said, looking up at his father. Tears streamed down his little face, but for the first time in a very long while his eyes blazed with hope. Angelique saw in his expression a new love and respect for his father.

Her gaze turned toward Joseph, and slowly she crept toward him. He held out his hand, and with a sigh of relief, she nestled her small hand in his broad callused palm. Meanwhile, Philippe and Marie met in the center of the room, and Angelique saw her mother gently touch her father's scarred face.

"Dominique was always troubled by the French and Indian wars," Spencer Wolfe said softly, "and it particularly grieved her when she heard that the English were trying to take over Grand Pre. She kept saying, 'It is the homeland of my people. God must touch the wicked hearts of those who would take our land away. . . .' " He fell silent, unable to say more.

Angelique knew what she wanted to say, but she hesitated. Should she press their luck and deliver the message that rose in her heart? She sucked in a deep breath.

"Claude told me once that his mother had a favorite

verse of Scripture. Would it be inappropriate if we read it now in her honor?"

Spencer Wolfe looked at her thoughtfully. Then he opened a drawer and pulled out a Bible. "This was Dominique's. I think it would be a fitting tribute if you read the passage."

He handed the Bible to Angelique. She could see the bookmark in the Old Testament, and although she knew the verse by heart, she opened the Bible to 2 Chronicles 7, verse 14. Yes, it was the verse Claude had told her about.

Angelique began to read softly, reverently:

" 'If my people, which are called by my name, shall humble themselves, and pray, and seek my face, and turn from their wicked ways; then will I hear from heaven, and will forgive their sin, and will heal their land.' "

Angelique finished the verse and looked across at her parents and Joseph, then again to Claude and Spencer Wolfe. Claude was looking up at his father with a radiant face, hugging him even harder. Spencer Wolfe touched his son's hair with such gentleness that Angelique took a step forward, then halted. Claude's hair was the color of his mother's hair, she knew that much. Obviously, Dominique had left a part of herself and her love here in this place.

Spencer looked back at them. "Go back to your homeland," he said gently. "And go with our blessings."

epilogue

Angelique and Joseph walked together across the snow-covered meadow. Although the wind that whipped from Minas Bay was cold on her cheeks, the deep love that filled and overflowed Angelique's heart coursed through her veins as they huddled closer together.

They passed under the bare limbs of the apple trees, and she smiled. Her thoughts were on spring—new life, new birth. Their thick boots crunched through the heavy snow, the sound deeper as they climbed the slight incline where violet-covered crocuses would come again when the winter was gone. Angelique would treasure the sea of purple that would be spread before them then—and one day their children would eat the apples from the apple trees.

Joseph stopped walking as they reached their new home; Angelique thought she could have found the way here if she were blindfolded. She knew the way the sun and the wind felt here, and she knew their homeland as one knows a best friend.

Joseph turned to Angelique, smoothing back the lock of dark hair that the wind had tossed onto her soft cheek. With the tenderness of one who has lost a precious treasure and then, amazingly, recovered it, his long finger lingered on her shining dark brown hair. He was one of the blessed few, as were Angelique and her parents. The dark silky hair was cold against his fingers, and he rubbed the strand of hair gently, smiling down into her upturned eyes, soft brown eyes that mirrored the love in her soul.

Her lips parted as she looked up at him. This time, neither one of them was dreaming. They were back in their beloved homeland and they were together at last. Their home was waiting for them, and they would have their whole lives to be together.

Just before he kissed her, she whispered to him, "Thank God, we're home. . . ."

A Letter To Our Readers

Dear Reader:

In order that we might better contribute to your reading enjoyment, we would appreciate your taking a few minutes to respond to the following questions. We welcome your comments and read each form and letter we receive. When completed, please return to the following:

Rebecca Germany, Fiction Editor
Heartsong Presents
PO Box 719
Uhrichsville, Ohio 44683

1. Did you enjoy reading *Look Homeward, Angel?*
   ❑ Very much. I would like to see more books by this author!
   ❑ Moderately
   I would have enjoyed it more if ________________

   ____

   ____

2. Are you a member of **Heartsong Presents**? Yes ❑ No ❑
   If no, where did you purchase this book? ______________

   ____

3. How would you rate, on a scale from 1 (poor) to 5 (superior), the cover design? ________________________

4. On a scale from 1 (poor) to 10 (superior), please rate the following elements.

_____ Heroine _____ Plot

_____ Hero _____ Inspirational theme

_____ Setting _____ Secondary characters

5. These characters were special because________________

____

____

6. How has this book inspired your life?________________

____

____

7. What settings would you like to see covered in future **Heartsong Presents** books?________________

____

____

8. What are some inspirational themes you would like to see treated in future books?________________

____

____

9. Would you be interested in reading other **Heartsong Presents** titles? Yes ❑ No ❑

10. Please check your age range:
   ❑ Under 18 ❑ 18-24 ❑ 25-34
   ❑ 35-45 ❑ 46-55 ❑ Over 55

11. How many hours per week do you read?________________

Name ____

Occupation ____

Address ____

City ________________ State ________ Zip ________